Please return / renew by date shown.
You can renew it at:
norlink.norfolk.gov.uk
or by telephone: 0844 800 8006
Please have your library card & PIN ready

23/8
4/9 28/9
16/10

123

H

Tough Justice

When Ike Durrel robs the bank at Arrow Bend and kidnaps the banker's daughter, Jack Lane is unexpectedly thrown a lifeline to survival or else face certain death. Realistically, going up against an outlaw like Durrel could have only one outcome. But circumstances are such for Jack Lane that the gamble, despite its probable end, is the only way out of his dire financial trouble.

All he has to do is survive in Indian country during an uprising, deal with and finally face up to Ike Durrel and his brother Ned so that he can rescue Emily Watts.

Against all the odds, Lane's mission is nearly close to completion when the biggest surprise of all comes. And he is pitched back into deadly danger.

Tough Justice

SKEETER DODDS

A Black Horse Western

ROBERT HALE · LONDON

Typeset by
Derek Doyle & Associates, Shaw Heath
Printed and bound in Great Britain by
Antony Rowe Limited, Wiltshire

CHAPTER ONE

As Jack Lane rode into Huntley he reckoned that if the town did not fall in on itself before he left, it would not be long after when it did. The town still had traces of better times, more respectable times but, hugging the border as it was, the constant outlaw traffic had changed Huntley from what had been a family town to one of sudden gunfire and lots of funerals. Those citizens who had not fled the town went about their business with shut eyes and deaf ears, hoping not to attract the attention of the desperadoes all round them.

Lane would have given Huntley a wide berth had he not hoped to get a pointer in Ike Durrel's direction. And he knew that asking questions about Durrel, one of the most evil-minded bastards riding the outlaw trails, might make Huntley the last place he would visit.

Lane swung his horse towards the saloon,

hitched it and went inside. Curious eyes watched him closely.

'That's a whole lotta dust on you, mister,' said one of the men lounging against the wall of the saloon. 'Been ridin' hard, huh?'

'How do you think my ass got this flat, friend?' Lane joked.

For most, the joke eased the tension. However, the man who had asked the question was not laughing, smarting as he was from the quick-lipped riposte.

'Would that be hardcase dust or law dust?' he enquired, his gaze taking in every inch of Jack Lane.

Lane ignored the man's question, and passed on.

'You deaf?' the man growled.

Lane figured that to convey an impression of toughness (and an impression it would only be), the only kind of man who would get respect around Huntley, he would have to stand up to the hardcase. He looked the man right in the eye.

'I ain't looking for trouble,' he said. 'But,' he shifted his stance, 'if you're pushing. . . ?'

The hardcase was taken aback, but recovered quickly. The men with him perked up, sensing entertainment to come.

'Know who I am?' the man grated.

'Don't much care,' Lane said, in a bored tone of

voice, hoping that he had not overplayed his hand. Because if the man called his bluff, he would most assuredly be dead in a second flat. Being a sodbuster, the sixgun on his hip had hammered more nails than it had shot bullets. And those bullets it had fired mostly went way wide of what they were supposed to hit. 'Ain't got all day, mister,' he said dismissively. Lane turned and strolled into the saloon, expecting any second to be challenged. However, no challenge came. Jack Lane reckoned that he was a much better actor than he had ever imagined. He strolled up to the bar. 'Whiskey.' While the barkeep poured, Jack Lane turned and let his gaze wander over the dozen or so imbibers. When he saw a man in a far corner, dishevelled and licking lips as dry as desert stone, Lane reckoned he had found a man who would answer his questions. 'I'll take the bottle,' he told the 'keep. He strolled to a table about midway between the bar and the drunk and sat down. Along the way he let his eyes meet the drunk's invitingly. A couple of minutes later the drunk joined him. When he sat at his table, Jack Lane shoved the bottle towards him. It was on his second drink that Lane reckoned that the drunk had thawed enough to be questioned.

'I'm looking for a fella called Ike Durrel,' Lane said. 'Can you point me, friend?'

The drunk's eyes popped. 'Ike Durrel! You must

want to die real fast, mister.' Lane poured another drink. 'Durrel's got a brother he hides out with. Near a place called Skull Hills. It's got other names, too. But round here that's the name it got after a wagon train was wiped out by the Apaches, who stuck every single skull on a pole as a warning to other whitefolk who might be of a mind to trespass on Indian land, not to.'

The drunk sighed wearily.

'You know, friend. If that wagon train had made it through a couple of years ago, this would have been a decent town instead of the shithole it's become.'

He looked at the near empty bottle.

'Another bottle and I'll draw you a map,' he offered.

Lane called for another bottle.

'You ain't law,' the drunk said. 'I'd know a lawman when I'd see one. Used to be marshal here.' He poured, gulped, and continued, 'And I figure that the sixgun on your hip is more for decoration than for shooting.'

Jack Lane shifted uneasily under the drunk's searching gaze and his astute assessment.

'A word of advice, friend,' the drunk said. 'Get outta this town, pronto. And don't tangle with Ike Durrel.'

Lane grinned. 'That's two words of advice.'

The drunk did not laugh.

'Ben Clark's the name' he said. 'And you know what, soon I'll pin on a badge again and run the scum out. Make it a family town again, like it used to be.'

'I reckon you will at that, Ben,' Jack Lane said kindly, not wanting to put any more hurt than there already was in the drunk's eyes.

Clark's enthusiasm quickly changed to suspicion, the way a drunk's does. 'You don't believe me, do you? You figure that Ben Clark's all washed up and done for. Well, you're wrong,' he said garrulously, focusing attention on the men across the saloon, the last thing Lane wanted. 'I'll show you. I'll show every damn one of you!' he shouted across the bar.

Clark pushed the glass he was supping from aside.

'That, mister, was Ben Clark's last drink.'

When the mocking laughter faded, a man moved away from the group. He was sporting a two-gun rig, the walnut handles of which were polished by frequent use. With a bottle of rotgut in each hand he swaggered up to the table with three other hardcases in tow.

'Now that sure is a real pity, *Marshal* Clark,' he sniggered. 'Guess I'm goin' to have to spill all this lovely liquor on the floor.'

The trio of hardcases backing him joined in his mockery of the drunk. The man uncorked one of the bottles and began pouring the liquor on to the floor. Ben Clark's agonized gaze followed the amber stream. 'Good liquor, Marshal.' Clark's tormentor waved the bottle under the drunk's nose.

The pain in Ben Clark's eyes was intense as he fought his demons, and tried to live up to his promise of a moment before.

Clark's taunter swallowed deeply from the bottle. Swishing the whiskey about his mouth, he let it trickle slowly down his chin.

Jack Lane knew that he should walk away, that what he was about to do was loco. He had already played one bluff, and this would probably be one bluff too many.

'Leave him be,' he intoned.

The hardcase turned mean eyes on Lane. 'Butt out, mister. Ain't none of your business.'

'Ben's a friend of mine,' Lane stated.

A warm glow lit Ben Clark's liquor deadened eyes.

'Friend, you say?' The hardcase flashed a look to his partners; a look that was more one of curiosity than terror. 'Got a monicker?'

'Frank Stiller,' Ben Clark said, authoritatively. 'Now, I'm sure you fellas don't want to lock horns with Frank Stiller.'

'Now, Ben,' Lane chuckled lazily, left with no alternative but to play along with Clark, 'don't go scaring these fine gents. I ain't as fast as I used to be.'

'Even ten times slower than you were, and you'd still be grease-lightning fast, Frank,' Clark said. 'You boys meant no harm, I'm sure.'

Lane was hoping that the quartet of hardcases would accept the olive branch Clark had held out. Three of them seemed to be of a mind to. But it was obvious that the hardcase who had made the running did not share their inclination.

However, luckily for Jack Lane, one of his backers piped up: 'We didn't mean no insult, Mr Stiller. Now did we, Ed?'

'We was just joshin',' a second of Ed's partners added.

'Yeah,' Ed said. 'Just joshin'.'

His partners' relief was immeasurable.

Ed's eyes were boring into Jack Lane, whose problem now was trying to figure out how Frank Stiller, whoever the hell he was, would react. He had never heard of Stiller, but obviously he was a man with a tough-as-nails reputation to have thrown a scare into the toerags who had been hell-bent on trouble. The wrong move now on his part could resurrect that trouble; trouble he was not equipped to deal with by a long shot.

'I figure that joshing is not a word I'd use to describe your hoggish attitude, mister,' Lane told the man called Ed. For the second time, Ben

Clark's eyes popped. 'I figure that an apology is still owing to Ben.'

'Apology?' Ed yelped. 'To a stinkin' drunk?'

Jack Lane set his features in what he hoped was stone, his eyes appropriately flinty like he was certain Frank Stiller's would have been, and prayed. He knew that if for a second the hardcases tumbled to the bluff Ben Clark had pulled, trouble would come hard and fast.

Ben Clark's eyes filled with regret for having put the kind stranger in the way of being killed. His mouth opened, Lane reckoned to acknowledge his bluff and take the blame on himself. Lane's hand shot out to grab Clark's arm to stymie his confession. There was no option but to continue the bluff, and hope that the hardcases would remain as convinced as they were.

Quick to spot Clark's reaction, Ed growled, 'You got somethin' to say, drunk? Spit it out.'

'Ben's out of this,' Lane barked. 'You deal with me.' Jack Lane stood up and kicked back the chair he had been seated on, in a fashion he had seen gunfighters assume in saloons. He dropped his hand to hover over his sixgun that was, as Ben Clark had so shrewdly observed, more a decoration than a practical shooting iron. 'If you've got a quarrel, it's with me.'

'You know who I am, Stiller?' Ed asked, obviously thinking that when he revealed his identity it would make a difference.

Jack Lane shrugged, as if he hadn't a care in the world.

'Don't make a difference who the hell you are, mister,' he declared. 'I've got your measure.'

'That a fact.' The hardcase shifted his stance to one of preparedness for gunplay. 'Well, the name's Ed Rekton.'

Lane struck a pose of indifference. He stepped back into a shadow to hide the sudden flush of perspiration on his brow. He had heard the name before, and always in connection with the vilest evil. Lane glanced at Rekton's backers, and of the trio he figured that two were Dan and Luke Rekton, and the other man who made up the Rekton outfit had to be Al Baker, a cousin of the Rektons, each of the four more evil than the other.

'Still want that apology, Stiller?' Ed Rekton's voice had the sing-song cockiness of the confident.

'It don't matter none, ah. . . .' Ben Clark's face fuzzed over.

'Seems that the drunk's forgotten your monicker,' Ed Rekton said, his suspicion going up several notches. 'Ain't that strange?' he asked his backers, who were also taking a new interest in Jack Lane.

'What do you expect,' Lane snorted. 'He's a drunk. His marbles are scattered every which way.'

'Frank,' Clark said, much to Jack Lane's relief.

'You're right, Frank. Rotgut's scattered my wits for sure.'

Would Rekton settle for a first name or push for Lane's fictitious surname which, Lane suspected, was as far away from Ben Clark's recollection as the moon is to earth. Ed Rekton seemed satisfied, but not so Al Baker.

'What's that feller's name again,' he quizzed Clark. 'The bit that comes after Frank.'

As Lane attempted to supply the information Baker had demanded of Clark, Ed Rekton snarled, 'You be still, mister!'

'Why, Stiller,' Clark announced, his befuddled brain prompted by the use of the word 'still'. 'Frank Stiller.'

Not having made the connection between Ed Rekton's unintentional prompt and Clark's confident response to Baker's interrogation, Baker relented.

Praying that he was playing his cards right, Jack Lane barked, 'Now, with that out of the way, you've got a choice, Rekton. You can apologize or draw.'

Lane was pleased to see that his bold stand had Rekton doubting. 'There's four of us, Stiller. I reckon that those are odds you can't beat.'

'Might be right at that,' Lane conceded, in a cavalier fashion. 'But you're a dead man standing,' he told Ed Rekton. 'Because my first bullet will go right to the centre of your heart. And, boys,' he continued, addressing the trio behind Ed Rekton, 'I think it only fair to point out that a couple of you are likely to go to hell with him.'

Ed Rekton's cockiness drained away like water through a holed bucket.

Seeing Ed Rekton's shakiness, Lane growled, 'Make your apology or make your play, Rekton. I tend to get real tetchy with a fella who can't make up his mind. Killed a couple of men in my time for keeping me waiting too long. And,' he glared at Ed Rekton, 'for a whole lot less dithering.' Jack Lane spread his legs in what he hoped was a classic gunfighter's stance. 'I'll count to three.

'One. . . .'

The Rektons' and Al Baker's astonishment turned to alarm.

'Two. . . .'

'Thr—'

'I'm surely sorry, Clark,' Ed Rekton piped up.

'Is that OK with you, Ben?' Lane asked the drunk.

'S-s-sure, Frank,' Clark stammered, once he had overcome his bewilderment.

'Then that's an end of the matter,' Lane said. 'I'm sure you fellas have got things to do elsewhere.'

Ed Rekton, ramrod stiff with indignation, led the way to the batwings. Lane's tension made it difficult to breathe, because he knew that a man who had to eat humble pie might at any second decide that he was going to spit it out. When they had gone Lane unholstered his sixgun to give himself a fighting chance if the Rektons and Baker turned back. Then, satisfied that they would not, Lane sat down at the table, glad that his legs had not turned to jelly as they had threatened to.

Ben Clark poured a drink and handed it to Lane.

'You need this more than me right now, friend,' he said.

Lane gratefully gulped down the whiskey. 'That fella Stiller sure put legs under those bastards,' he said. 'Who is he, anyway?'

Ben Clark looked blankly at Jack Lane, grinning broadly. 'Don't know.'

'Don't know?'

'No. The name sounded just about right, I reckoned.'

Jack Lane blanched. He shoved his glass at Clark. 'Don't spare it. I need every drop to stop the shakes I've been holding at bay.'

Jack Lane rode out of Huntley in possession of the map Clark had drawn for him of the route to Ike Durrel's hideout, his brother Ned's horse ranch, where the outlaw took refuge when the heat on him was too much. When Clark handed over the map he had again advised Lane to forget about Durrel.

'You don't stand a chance, Lane,' he predicted.

16

'You'll be riding through Indian country. If the Apaches don't get your hair, Durrel will do for you.'

Lane knew that the most probable outcome of his folly was the fulfilment of Ben Clark's prediction; a prediction which had also been voiced by Charlie Brady, the marshal of Arrow Bend, from where he had set out. He was a sodbuster, and in no way equipped to tangle with either Indians or Ike Durrel.

Jack Lane had a choice. He could forget about Ike Durrel and keep his scalp. Or he could risk losing his hair or being killed by Durrel, in the hope of collecting the $2000 bounty on Durrel he was chasing.

While he pondered his options and weighed the risks, Jack Lane drew rein a spit short of the canyon marking the beginning of Indian territory. He could turn tail and forget the bounty (money that would be the difference between survival and going under) that Lucas Watts the Arrow Bend banker had offered him to rescue his kidnapped daughter Emily from Ike Durrel's clutches.

'I'll also cancel your debt to the bank,' Watts had promised.

If he turned tail now, the future would be as bright as a rusty nickel.

Horse sense kicking in, the mare shuffled restlessly and looked back at Lane with wide eyes.

17

Lane could not figure out whether the mare was frightened, or trying to figure out whether her rider was loco. Probably a little of both, he concluded.

'We've come this far, horse,' he said. 'Let's go get that critter Ike Durrel.'

He set off down the shale track that led into the canyon, the mare's unease growing with every passing second, as was her rider's.

CHAPTER TWO

'If you do, it'll be a damn fool thing to do,' had been Marshal Charlie Brady's opinion of what he considered to be the most loco idea he had ever heard. 'You're a sodbuster, Jack. You ain't got the know-how to tangle with a fella like Ike Durrel.

'Might as well shoot yourself now and get it over with, I reckon.'

Charlie Brady's words drifted back to Lane; words spoken when he was thinking about taking Lucas Watts up on his offer.

The reason he had a raw butt, in country that any whiteman (except men like Ike Durrel) with a modicum of sense would stay well clear of, was that in a third year of almost no rain the soil on his farm had turned to powder.

'Pay up or move out,' had been Lucas Watts's initial heartless ultimatum. Lane had pleaded for time, but pleading with a banker was like trying to wring teardrops from a stone. 'I've been patient,

Lane,' Watts had pointed out, and there was no denying the truth of his statement. 'But I've got to close the book on this loan sooner rather than later.'

'A lot of folk are owing, Mr Watts,' he had argued, in a last throw of the dice.

'That's the problem, Lane. The bank has got to realize the assets tied up in outstanding loans to stay afloat.'

'Who're you going to sell to, if no one's got money to buy?' Jack Lane had hotly challenged the banker.

'Fact is, I'm thinking of going back East,' Lucas Watts said. He groaned. 'Why I ever got the notion to come West I'll never know. I can't sell a bank with a load of bad debts. The only hope I have is to have lots of assets on my books to tempt another banker with more resources than I have to buy me out and hold out until things pick up round here, when he'll be able to get a good price for farms like yours, Lane. Arrow Bend will take years to come back. I can't hold out, Lane.'

Watts had sighed wearily.

'I'm only hoping that I can find a buyer at all. Besides, I'm a widower with a daughter who'll be a woman soon. Back East, she'll stand a better chance of finding a suitable husband.'

Jack Lane had heard the stories going round town about Emily Watts's hankering for Cy

Locklin, handsome as they come with the kind of roguish charm that could turn any woman's head, but rotten through and through.

'Em'ly likes the bad ones,' Charlie Brady had told Lane. 'It's a full-time job for me to keep the likes of Cy Locklin from cornering her.'

'It's not easy for a man to bring up a girl properly without the soft hand of a woman, Lane,' Lucas Watts had said, tiredly. 'Back East my sister will replace Emily's mother, and I'll be able to sleep nights again. You've got three weeks, Lane,' he had finished brusquely, and slammed the ledger on his desk shut.

As Lane was leaving the bank, heavy-shouldered and gloomy of spirit, he had stepped aside to let two men enter. 'Thank you kindly, sir,' one of the men said, the man he came to know as Ike Durrel. Five minutes later the main street was being peppered with lead as Durrel and his partner came rushing from the bank after heisting it.

It was almost closing time and Emily Watts had come to the bank to walk her pa home as she usually did. She was in the wrong place at the wrong time. Durrel took her hostage. No one was expecting the bank of a burg on its knees to be robbed, and in the main the citizens of Arrow Bend were not given to wearing guns. They were therefore not of a mind to argue with flying lead. And the only man who would or could mount a challenge to the bank robbers, Marshal Charlie Brady, was out of town standing between ranchers who were willing to murder each other for what little water was left in a creek.

Fate took a hand in matters that morning to claim the life of Durrel's sidekick. The team of a wagon outside the general store, upset by the wholly unnecessary lead-slinging, took fright and charged across the outlaws' escape route. Durrel, obviously the better horseman, veered away to round the wagon, but his partner rode straight in to it and became impaled on a shaft of the wagon. The awful horror of what had happened held the townsfolk in the grip of shock. But not so Ike Durrel. The cruel fate of his partner did not trouble him in the least.

'That man's got Emily!'

All eyes went to Lucas Watts, wringing his hands outside the bank. With everyone intent on staying clear of the flying lead, no one had realized until Watts cried out that Durrel had kidnapped Emily Watts. With the marshal out of town and having to be summoned back, and with no deputy to stand in for him, the organizing of a posse took too long.

'Durrel could be at the end of the territory by now!' Brady had complained when he arrived back in town. He headed the posse for three days before giving up on catching Durrel. 'Probably across the damn border by now,' he had reasoned.

'Nothing we could do, Charlie,' the livery owner had complained in turn. 'A posse without your say-so ain't got any legal standing.'

'Legal standing,' the Arrow Bend lawman had yelled. 'The territorial governor would have pinned medals on the men who ran Ike Durrel to ground. Once he hit the trail with hours to spare, picking up Durrel's trail would have been difficult enough. After almost a day, we might as well be chasing a damn ghost!'

On seeing the posse return without Emily, Lucas Watts had collapsed and was in Doc Larson's care at his infirmary.

'Gibbering,' Larson had told anyone who enquired after the banker's health. 'Could spend the rest of his life making no sense, so severe has his shock been.'

Charlie Brady had telegraphed towns between Arrow Bend and the border, which he reckoned Durrel was headed for by any one of a hundred trails. He was counting on some lawman having the grit in his belly to act if he saw Durrel. But in reality he reckoned that once his telegraph was received, every sheriff and marshal would find some other urgent business to make himself scarce until Ike Durrel had come and gone. And who could blame them. Ike Durrel was the meanest bastard that ever came down the line.

'There's got to be something that can be done,

Charlie,' Lane said, when Brady made his views known to him.

'Yeah. There is. Pray that Ike Durrel will tire quickly of Emily Watts,' Brady had said glumly.

'There's got to be something that can be done,' Lucas Watts repeated a couple of days later when the shock loosened its hold on him and his reason returned, and he did not hold out any hope that Brady's alerting of other town lawmen would be of benefit. 'What we need, Marshal, is. . . .'

'Is?' Brady prompted, when the banker became lost in thought.

'. . . A man who stands to lose everything he's worked for,' Lucas Watts said.

'I'm not sure I catch your drift, Mr Watts,' said the Arrow Bend lawman.

And that was where Jack Lane came into the picture.

CHAPTER THREE

'Someone's coming, Jack,' Martha Lane said, shaking her husband from the after dinner doze he had fallen into.

'At this time of night?' Lane questioned, doubtfully. Then he heard the wheels of a rig in the yard. 'You stay put, honey,' he had told his wife, taking a rifle from the rack just inside the door, 'while I go and check out our night visitor.'

'Be careful, Jack,' Martha fretted. 'I don't want to be a widow woman.'

Heeding his wife's advice, Lane, normally a man who was direct in his approach, opened the door a crack to vet his nocturnal visitor. His neck of the woods, not having much in the way of prosperity to attract hardcases, was tamer than other parts of the territory. However, the wise man always allowed for strays who, in passing, might just be mean-minded enough to vent their spleen on the nearest to them.

Jack Lane's surprise was total when he set eyes on Lucas Watts. Being a poor farmer, he never had visitors of the banker's social standing.

'Watts!' was Martha Lane's stunned reaction when her husband told her who their caller was. 'What the heck is he prowling round at dead of night for?'

'One way to find out.' Lane pulled open the door. 'Mr Watts,' he greeted the banker pleasantly. 'Mighty nice of you to drop by, sir.'

'This is not a social visit, Lane,' the banker replied curtly. 'I've got a proposition to put to you which, if you take it, will solve all your problems.'

'That's mighty interesting to hear, sir.'

Lane stepped aside to let the banker enter, just as Martha Lane dashed from the bedroom, having ditched her apron and tidied her hair.

'Why, Mr Watts.' She beamed. 'How nice it is to see you.'

Lucas Watts's curtness continued.

'If you'll leave us, Mrs Lane. I've got business with your husband.'

Martha Lane's face, flushed with excitement, paled on hearing the banker's summary dismissal, because she feared the worst. Jack had made her aware of the hopeless nature of his meeting with the banker. Therefore, she could only think of one possible reason for Watts's visit, and that was to give them a foreclosure date.

'Sure, Mr Watts,' she said despondently, and began to back away towards the bedroom.

'Now just wait a minute, Watts!' Jack Lane barked. 'You stay right where you are, Martha.' The farmer came toe to toe with the banker to deliver an ultimatum. 'This is my home, and Martha is my wife. And if you don't want to show due respect, Watts, you can turn tail right now.'

Martha Lane staggered weakly, fearing that her husband's tirade would only make the banker meaner than he already was.

'Is that understood?' Lane demanded.

The banker's apology was immediate.

'I'm sorry, Lane – Mrs Lane. I displayed the manners of a hog. Perhaps it would be best if you joined us, ma'am. Because what I've come to say will, I'm sure, concern you as much as your husband.'

Martha sank on to a chair at the table, her heart constricted. Jack Lane invited the banker to sit and then sat himself. Watts's shoulders were weighed down by the terrible burden of his daughter's kidnapping, and he had aged at least ten years.

'Lane,' he began, 'I'm not a man given to time-wasting. So I'll come straight to the point. You owe the bank.' Watts held up his hand to stay Jack Lane's protest or plea. 'Find my daughter and bring her home safely to me, and I will wipe out your debt and give you two thousand dollars' bounty.'

Jack Lane's jaw had dropped.

'Now, I don't expect you to say ay or nay right now.' He stood up to leave. 'But I'd appreciate your answer by opening time at the bank tomorrow.'

'What about the posse?' Lane asked. 'Charlie Brady said he'd ride out again if Durrel wasn't nailed between Arrow Bend and the border.'

'Posses are big and unwieldy, Lane. While lawmen in towns between here and the border will run like scared jackrabbits. So, I figure that one man riding alone might just track Durrel more effectively. A lone rider will be able to move faster to start with.'

Watts stood up.

'I'll leave you good people now. I hope to see you tomorrow, Lane. I figure that you're my last hope of ever being united with my daughter again.'

When standing, Lucas Watts appeared to be several inches shorter; the hunch of worry did that to a man, Lane knew.

He had had more than his fair share of worries since the end of the war. At first he'd drifted, like so many other men who had suddenly found themselves with nothing to do now that the war had ended. Until one day, down near the border, he set foot in a town called Lucky Drift, arriving just as the stage pulled in. He had idly perused the stage on route to the saloon which had been his first stop in a long litany of towns, hoping to sit in on a game of poker or blackjack in the hope that his luck would give him enough of a pot to yet again move on to another town, another saloon, and the hope of a winning streak again. He knew, like most men wasting away their days searching for something they were not even sure they would recognize if and when they found it, that one day he would run out of towns and luck.

And that's when he saw Martha Carey, stepping from the stage, looking around her for someone who was not there to greet her. In seconds she was exhibiting the signs of panic. 'Need help, ma'am?' he had enquired of her.

She had turned away, but not before her look told him what she thought he was, and what she thought he was after. He could understand, of course. A young lady, alone, in a town where decent folk were in short supply and toerags ten to the dime had every right to be nervous. He had already noticed the way the saloon keeper was sizing up the young woman, obviously seeing in her a new addition to his jaded string of doves.

'You really do need help, ma'am,' Lane had

insisted, picking up her luggage.

'Put that valise right back where you found it!' she berated him. 'I'll have you know that my young man is meeting me.' She looked to the dusty trail leading out of Lucky Drift, empty of any presence all the way to the purple foothills in the distance. 'He'll be along any minute now.' There was more hope in her voice than certainty. 'And when he does, he'll give you a good thrashing, if you persist in bothering me.'

Tiring of her rejection, Jack Lane had dropped her bags. 'Pardon me, ma'am,' he said. 'I surely don't want to be a bother.' As he walked away, the saloon-keeper made his move, his smile pure snake oil. Jack Lane told himself that he had tried to help, and that there was nothing more he could do.

'I'm sure that young man of yours won't be long more, miss,' said the saloon keeper, with the hiss of snake. 'I'd like to offer you the hospitality of a room while you're waiting.' He held out a soft hand that had never seen hard work. 'The name's Harry Stone, ma'am.'

Martha Carey had shot Lane a smug look, before accepting Stone's offer. 'Thank you, sir. I can see that at least there's one gentleman in this town.'

'A young lady has to be careful,' Stone advised, turning to cast a knowing sneer Lane's way. Stone called a lackey to take her bags, while he offered his arm to the young woman. 'Might I ask the name of the young tyro you're expecting?'

'His name is Stan Wright, sir. Works for the Dusty Hollow ranch. Do you know him?'

'Surely do. A fine young feller.'

Martha Carey smiled ear to ear. 'I think so, too, Mr Stone.'

At the batwings, Martha had swept past Lane without as much as a glance for a mangy dog. Stone sneered again. Jack Lane kept telling himself that what was happening was none of his business. He was in Lucky Drift to play cards and drink whiskey.

'Our finest room, I think, Miss. . . ?'

'Carey, Mr Stone. Martha Carey.'

'And while you're resting, I'll send someone out to the Dusty Hollow to tell your young man that you've arrived. Although how he could be so careless in missing the stage, I simply cannot understand, Miss Carey.'

'Oh, please, sir. You must call me Martha.'

'Martha,' the saloon owner purred, much as the snake in the Garden of Eden must have. 'I'm sure we'll be *real* good friends.'

'I have no doubt that we will be, Mr Stone.'

Harry Stone smiled beatifically. 'And you must call me Harry, Martha.'

Martha Carey had blushed. 'Why that's mighty kind of you . . . Harry.'

'Harry's ringed another,' sniggered one of the men at the blackjack table at which Jack Lane was pulling up a chair.

'Might, if I'm lucky, spend some of my winnin's on a trip upstairs,' said a second man.

A third man at the table opined, 'You'd better win fast, Huey. Otherwise, I reckon that you'll be at the tail end of a long queue. Harry ain't a feller to let a gold-mine like her stay unworked for very long.'

'Spence,' Stone called to a man lounging against the bar, a .45 slung low on his right hip, tied down in the fashion of a man with a regular use for the Colt. 'Take Martha's bags upstairs.'

The mean-eyed man called Spence made no secret of his displeasure at being called on to do the chores – his talents and usefulness lay elsewhere.

'Barrett sure don't like what he's bein' asked to do,' said the man who had commented on Stone's quick use of Martha Carey.

'Might get real interestin' round here, Andy,' commented the first man at the table who had spoken.

Stone, obviously perturbed by the hardcase's spit-quick lack of compliance with his request, said, 'Don't keep the lady waiting, Spence.' He turned away from Martha Carey and glared snake-eyed at his hireling.

Spence Barrett delayed another couple of seconds while he tossed back his whiskey before crossing the saloon and, sourly grabbing Martha Carey's valise, brushed past her and led the way upstairs, taking the stairs two steps at a time, making Martha scurry after him.

'You'll be sure to send someone out to the Dusty Hollow to tell Stan that I'm here, won't you, Harry?'

'Right away, Martha,' he promised falsely.

'You've been so kind,' said Martha Carey. 'And such a gentleman, too,' she added, her critically contemptuous gaze settling on Jack Lane. With a toss of her red mane, she continued on upstairs.

'Sure is your lucky day, Harry,' said one of the card-players.

'Bet you never expected such an earner to step off the stage and into your hands,' the man called Andy chuckled.

'You fellas playing cards or gossiping like old women?'

All eyes switched to Jack Lane, trying to understand why he was so riled. Harry Stone gave them the answer.

'This gent tried to beat me to the prize, fellas,' he informed them. 'Got a kick in the butt for his trouble.'

'You figure she's intact?' The question had come from a man in a fancy waistcoat seated in the far corner of the saloon.

'Untouched, I figure,' was Stone's opinion. 'You interested, mister?'

'Maybe.'

'A first-timer, as opposed to my regulars, comes at top dollar,' Stone said, his eyes taking in every inch of the man. 'But I reckon you've got the shekels to meet my price.'

'Ain't fair, Harry,' Andy said. 'Givin' first taste to a stranger, 'bove regulars who've had to put up with your worn-out stable of doves.'

The other men at the card table joined in the protest, as did several others scattered around the saloon.

Stone was pragmatic.

'I run my business on the best profit I can make,' he said, giving no concession. 'Match the stranger's dollars, plus, and the highest bidder gets first bedding. Simple as that, gents.'

'You know we can't match the fancy Dan's poke,' Andy protested.

'How d'ya know?' Stone's gaze went to the smartly dressed man. 'He ain't made me an offer yet. You making an offer, mister?'

The man got up and whispered in Stone's ear. Immediately the brothel keeper's eyes popped. 'For that much you can bed her for as long as you want,' he said, gleefully.

'Wonder how she'll like hearin' that Stan Wright

is boxed over in the undertaker's, ready for worm-feed. Put there by Spence Barrett on your say-so, Stone,' the man called Andy griped.

Jack Lane had been stunned by the revelation. Two men at the end of the bar took the nod from Harry Stone. They grabbed the man called Andy, hauled him to the door and slung him out.

'Bother Mr Stone again, and you'll be joining Wright,' the taller of Stone's toerags threatened.

The schomozzle over with, Stone quickly got back to business.

'She's yours for as long as you want,' he told Martha Carey's first customer. A considerable fee changed hands. 'Enjoy yourself,' Stone crowed, as the man went to go upstairs. 'What room is she in?' Stone enquired of Spence Barrett who was coming back downstairs.

'Number three. Facing the street.'

'Why don't you go back upstairs and smooth the way for our friend, Spence?'

Barrett did not hesitate to do as Stone asked. Obviously, allowing respectable young women to be violated was a line of work he considered fitting.

'Obliged,' said the fancy Dan, his eyes already glittering with his thoughts of the pleasures to come.

At the card table, Jack Lane threw in his hand. 'I guess this game is about done for me.' He stood up and strolled out of the saloon. Once outside, his pace quickened considerably. He ran into the alley alongside the saloon and raced up the stairs that most saloons had for clients who wanted the services the saloon had to offer, but not the notoriety of going through the main door, and entered the upstairs through a window at the end of the hallway, just in time to see Spence Barrett entering a room, presumably room number three. The man followed him in. Lane could hear muted voices at first, but then came Martha Carey's strident protestation. A second later she flung open the room door and ordered the men out. Barrett grabbed her by the hair and flung her back into the room.

'You do as this gent wants,' he growled. 'Or I'll damn well slit your throat. You're bought and paid for, woman!'

Martha Carey protested again, and Lane grimaced as he heard the sound of a fist meeting flesh. Martha screamed out. The room door opened and Spence Barrett stepped into the hall, massaging his knuckles.

'I reckon she'll do anything you want now,' he said, talking back into the room to the fancy Dan. 'And if she don't, I'll come back up here and really lay in to her!' he promised.

'Stan Wright will—'

'Do nothin', lady,' Barrett scoffed. 'It's real difficult for a man in a pine box to do anything.'

Jack Lane heard Martha Carey's shocked intake of breath.

'Stan is dead?' she had asked, as if unable to take in Barrett's news.

'Yeah. I know, 'cause I killed him only a coupla hours ago.'

'Why?'

'Old man Riley, the owner of the Dusty Hollow, ain't got no kin to pass on his ranch to. So Stan Wright became the son he never had. Now, Mr Stone has his eye on the Dusty Hollow, as he has on most things in Lucky Drift and hereabouts, but old man Riley wouldn't sell to him. Mr Stone figured that that would change if Wright was no longer around.'

Spence Barrett guffawed.

'Right now you've got other things to worry about, Miss high-and-mighty.'

Stone's lackey slammed the room door shut and headed downstairs tossing a silver dollar, feeling pleased with himself.

Jack Lane had made his way quickly along to room number three and did not hesitate to kick in the door when he heard Martha Carey scream. The fancy Dan had her pinned to the bed, his hands ripping her clothing. Lane grabbed him by the hair and yanked his head back. In one swift, angry movment he propelled the would-be rapist across the room and through the window. The man screamed all the way down to the street. Landing head first, the crown of his skull burst like rotten fruit and his brains poured out on to the dusty street.

'We've got to get out of here, and fast,' Lane said, helping Martha Carey to legs that were absolute jelly. He lifted her into his arms, and was in the hall when Spence Barrett bounded upstairs. Seeing Jack Lane, he went for his gun. But, Lane, having taken the precaution to draw his pistol, had the advantage over the hardcase and did not hesitate to use it. Barrett glanced down at the gaping hole in his chest, screamed with his last breath, and toppled back downstairs. The toerag who had chucked the card-player who had criticized Stone's lack of loyalty to his regulars, appeared at the end of the stairs. This time Jack Lane's shot was not as deadly, but the bullet did rip a chunk from the mahogany stairs, sizeable and pointed enough to take most of the hardcase's cheek with it as it spun past him. He howled like an animal in a trap and danced about.

He heard Stone order his other gun-handler to challenge Lane, but the sound of running feet across the saloon floor was evidence of his unwillingness to follow his partner. 'You bastard coward!' Stone raged from downstairs. A gun exploded and the running feet stopped.

Jack Lane had hurried Martha along the hall to the door at its end. Her shock abating, thankfully her legs now had more strength, which made Lane's task easier. By the time they reached the alley she was outpacing him in her urgency to get away from the scene of her ordeal. On reaching the end of the alley, Lane pulled her back.

'You'll run right into a bullet,' he had told her as she fought him, so anxious was she to see the back of Lucky Drift.

Jack Lane edged up to the corner of the alley to reconnoitre the main street. It was deserted. Maybe, having lost his henchmen, Harry Stone was lying low. On the other hand, he might be waiting to line Lane up in his gunsights. He looked across the street to the sheriff's office where a man, the badge-toter he reckoned, was displaying no interest or eagerness to get involved. Either he was a coward, or, more likely, on Stone's payroll, Lane reckoned.

'Wait here while I grab a couple of nags,' he told Martha.'

'I'm coming with you,' she said, resolutely.

Lane was about to argue with her, but the set of her jaw told him that he'd be wasting precious time that he did not have.

'OK,' he agreed. 'Ready?'

'Ready,' she confirmed.

Lane sprinted from the alley across the street to a pair of waiting horses hitched to the rail outside the general store. A couple of token shots came from the batwings of the saloon. But when Lane crouched and returned lead, shattering the saloon window, the shooting stopped and their departure from Lucky Drift was thereafter unimpeded. They kept riding at a gallop until Lane, seeing no dust trail behind him, drew rein.

'I guess we're home and free now,' he said.

Her terrifying ordeal over, Martha Carey had begun to weep in great heaving sobs. Jack Lane recalled how much at a loss he had been then. Flying lead was one problem; a problem he had had many times before in his drifting life style. But having a weeping woman on his hands was something else. All he could do was wait until Martha Carey had cried herself dry, when she asked:

'What now?'

That was a question that took three more days to be answered. By that time, they were talking vaguely about him settling down, and the possibility that they could start a farm together. When that idea was more or less agreed on, the next problem was that living together would not be right and proper without a band of gold on Martha's wedding finger.

40

'Ain't you too upset about having lost Stan Wright?' he had enquired of Martha, curiously.

'Never saw him. So what I haven't had, I can't miss,' she said pragmatically.

'Never saw him?'

'Never set eyes on him,' Martha had confirmed. 'I reckon I'd better be totally honest with you, Jack.'

'I figure that would be nice, Martha,' he'd said.

'I'm a mail-order bride.'

'I'll be darned,' had been Jack Lane's response. 'Thought all mail-order brides were prunes and coyote ugly.' Then he had laughed, and that laughter rang back over the years to him now as he recalled. 'But I guess not all, huh?'

'What's tickling your ribs, Jack Lane?' Martha asked, as she sat by the fire rocking back and forth, nervously contemplating the offer Lucas Watts had just made to her husband. 'I don't see anything to laugh about in Lucas Watts's proposition. It would be darned suicide to take it up, and that's for sure. Might as well put a snake in your pocket as tangle with Ike Durrel.'

Jack Lane had not yet got around to giving serious consideration to the banker's offer, and he had planned on a more leisurely discussion about it with Martha. But, true to form, she had not minced her words.

'If I did manage to nail Durrel, it would get us out of the bind we're in,' Lane reasoned. 'Give us breathing space while we plan our next move, Martha.'

'A dead man's got no future, Jack,' she stated bluntly. 'You're a farmer. What the heck do you know about guns and hunting down men of Ike Durrel's ilk?'

'I can shoot straight,' Lane reminded his wife a tad huffily, and added self-consciously, 'Well, almost.'

'Sure, you can, *almost*,' she snorted. 'When you can take your time. Men like Ike Durrel don't give a man time, Jack. He can probably draw and shoot faster than a rattler can spit.'

'I rescued you OK from the clutches of Harry Stone,' Lane pointed out.

'Luck, Jack,' she pronounced. 'But luck like that don't come calling very often. And why you? I'll tell you why. Because no one else would touch Watts's proposition.'

'Ya know, Martha, you're doing my pride no good at all!' Lane complained.

'It ain't your pride I'm worried about. I don't want to be a widow woman.' She smiled fondly. 'Besides, I think you're kind of cute.'

'Yeah?'

'Yes. And you're a fair enough bed-warmer.'

'A bed-warmer!'

'And, to boot, I'm carrying, Jack.' Jack Lane was stunned. They had been married for seven years and had given up on having children. 'I reckon I'm in my third month. Now, would you want your boy to be without a daddy?'

'My boy?'

'What else? That's what you wanted, wasn't it. And I aim to please.'

Jack Lane grabbed his wife and danced her around the room until she was breathless, then he fretted, 'Ain't done harm, have I?'

'I don't reckon so.'

'A boy,' he marvelled. 'That starts a man thinking long term, don't it.'

Worried that her heady prediction of delivering a son might not come to pass, Martha Lane's face clouded. 'It might be a girl, Jack,' she cautioned. 'It's only a feeling I have that it's a boy. But maybe I'm wrong.'

She relaxed on seeing her husband's wide grin.

'A girl will do fine, too, honey,' he said.

'You're sure?' she checked.

'Sure am, woman. Boy or girl is God's gift, Martha.'

'You know,' she began, dewy-eyed, 'I can't say that I'm glad that Stan Wright was gunned down in Lucky Drift. But I'm more than glad that out of evil came good when I met you, Jack Lane.'

'Shucks, Martha. You'll have me blushing.'

43

'If you'd care to step into the bedroom, I'll make you blush like you've never blushed before,' she teased him.

'Leave the lamp off and I can hide my blushes.'

She looped her arm through his and drew him towards the bedroom.

'Not a chance,' she said. 'I want to feast my eyes on every blushing inch of you.'

Togged off and stark naked, Lane joked, 'Don't know why I spoil you like I do, wife.'

Breathless, and ever thrilled at the sight of her husband's trim and hard-muscled body, Martha reached for him, eager for him to take her. Long after, when Martha was asleep, Jack Lane found sleep elusive. After the heady excitement of first discovering that he was going to be a father, followed by the long and heart-palpitating frenzy of yet again discovering every inch of Martha's body, worry about the future returned and now his concern was even greater than it had been, knowing that another generation would soon be looking to him to secure the future.

Before going to sleep he had wanted to talk about Lucas Watts's offer. But on the few words that had been exchanged between him and Martha on the subject, it was clear that it was a proposition that was now dead in the water. She had talked about moving on. About how there was plenty of work in the cities of the East. But he was a farmer – a Western man, and he could not imagine ever living in a place full of the noise of commerce and people at every turn, with the sunset a weak and watery affair to be viewed over rooftops, instead of watching it majestically sink behind purple heathered hills.

When at last he dozed he slept uneasily, his dreams dark and dreary. After a moody breakfast, during which he reckoned Martha had little difficulty in reading his troubled thoughts, he readied himself to go to town to give Lucas Watts his answer as he had promised he would.

When he was saddled up, Martha said, 'You're doing the right thing, Jack. You'll be a family man soon.' Her remarks were proof positive of how accurately she had read his thoughts. 'You'll get to like Boston.' Heck, she had already decided where they were headed for. 'I spent a spell there before coming West as a mail-order bride.'

She looked into the empty vastness and pulled the shawl round her shoulders as a sudden breeze blew up, and he could see in her look the longing to be away for someplace she considered to be more civilized. And for the first time, Jack Lane wondered whether he had married the right woman in Martha Carey?

As he rode away she called after him, 'Check

with the general store if Mr Draper got in that yellow calico I was asking about. I'll want to look my Boston best when we arrive there.'

He waved in acknowledgement, not trusting his voice to keep secret his emotions; feelings that wiped away the excitement and jubilation of the night before, and the hope that Lucas Watts's visit had given him of being able to survive as a sodbuster until his fortunes turned, which he was sure would be soon.

But then he thought glumly, that he had spent five years waiting for his fortunes to turn, always feeling that a change of luck was just around the corner. Maybe, he thought, Boston would not be too bad. If a man put his mind to it, he could get used to most things. And how could he disappoint Martha. Take away from the glow that emanated from her when ever she thought about going back East.

He rode on, his mood switching between optimism and depression. Upon his arrival in Arrow Bend, Charlie Brady stepped from the marshal's office to cut his path.

'Howdy, Jack,' the lawman greeted in that fashion that made him eternally cheery. 'Got an early start, ain't ya?'

'Got to see Lucas Watts, Charlie.'

'Watts, huh? What about?'

Jack Lane snorted. 'You're a lousy liar, Charlie

46

Brady. And I reckon that it wasn't by chance you cut my path just now.'

'Sure, I heard Watts paid you a visit. I heard, too, why he did. And I've got to shoot straight from the hip, Jack. You'd be loco to take Watts up on his offer. At least a dozen lawmen and double that amount of bounty hunters have tried to hogtie Ike Durrel. Those who aren't dead are mostly crippled. It would be easier to tie a can to Satan's horns than take on Durrel single-handed.

'When Ike Durrel is finally brought to book, it'll take a strong-willed posse to do it.'

His sigh was long and weary.

'And to boot, even with a dozen men in the saddle against him, Durrel will still have to make a mistake.'

'All men make mistakes, Charlie,' Lane said. 'But you needn't worry. I'm turning down Watts' offer.'

Marshal Charlie Brady was visibly relieved. 'Drop by when you're done with Watts. I've got a bottle of Kentucky rye I've been keeping the cork on for the right occasion. I figure this is it.'

'I surely will, Charlie,' Lane promised. 'I've got a lot to celebrate. Martha's with child.'

'That's the darnest best news my ears have heard for a heck of a long time, Jack,' the lawman enthused. Aware that the Lanes had more or less given up on having a family, Brady was genuinely pleased with his long-time friend's news.

'A boy, Martha reckons,' Lane said proudly.

'Yeah? You'll be strutting like a damn peacock, I reckon.'

'Be seeing you in a couple of minutes,' Lane said, riding on to the banker's house at the end of the main street, the biggest and the finest in Arrow Bend. Not that there was much to beat. Watts came to the door to meet Lane, anxiety etched in every line of his face, which seemed to have reached a hundred years old since his daughter had been kidnapped by Ike Durrel.

'Well?' Watts anxiously enquired of Jack Lane.

'I'm real sorry, Mr Watts,' Lane said. 'But I can't take you up on your offer.'

Watts scowled. 'In that case I want you off your farm immediately, Lane.'

Shocked, Jack Lane pleaded, 'I've got to have time, Mr Watts. I just can't up and leave at the drop of a hat.'

'You've had your chance to keep your farm and get money in your pocket to hold out until things get better. You didn't take it. And I'm clean out of sympathy. I'll expect you gone by tomorrow.'

Watching from along the street, Charlie Brady could sense that Lane's decision not to take the banker's offer had served to make his problems worse than they already were. Watts was now gesticulating like a crazy man, and it was obvious that Jack Lane's pleading was cutting no ice. Watts went indoors, and the slam of his front door reverberated in the stillness of the morning.

Slumped in his saddle, Lane made his way back along the street and rode right past Charlie Brady who, not knowing what to say or what to do, let him go. Later, he'd ride out to the Lane place and offer his friend the $500 he had hidden under the floorboards in his parlour. It was every cent he had, and it would not make a dent in what Lane owed the bank, but it was all he could do. Another time he would have had a word in the banker's ear on Lane's behalf in his capacity as the chairman of the town council. But right now the banker was too out of his mind with worry about his daughter for him to listen to reason.

Jack Lane was nearing the end of the main street when Watts came from his house and hailed him. 'Another thousand dollars, Lane,' he called out.

Lane drew rein betwixt and between. A small part of his mind had already been regretting having rejected the banker's offer, while at the same time he knew the sense of what Martha had said about her being a widow and a child not having a pa. But if he managed to snare Durrel and rescue Emily Watts, all his worries would be over. The sale of his farm, added to Watts's cash would make it possible for him to move to better land at the other side of the mountain where the valley was cut by a river that bubbled up from deep within the earth and always flowed. It was good crop-growing country. There he could build a farm that would pass to his son and his sons again. For Martha, he could build a proper house instead of the cabin they now occupied.

Marshal Charlie Brady could see the wheels spinning in Lane's head.

'You'd be loco to take Watts's offer, Jack,' he counselled.

'Don't reckon I have a choice, Charlie,' was Lane's response. 'His bounty will make it possible to buy good land.'

'You go after Ike Durrel, and the only land you'll have is the grave he'll put you in, Jack. Right now Martha needs you.'

'Maybe it won't take long to run Durrel to ground, Charlie. Meantime, you'd look out for Martha, wouldn't you?'

'Looking out for Martha would be a privilege I don't deserve. But as far as I can, I'll see she'll want for nothing. But I still say that you're crazy to even think about hunting down Durrel.'

'Well, Lane?' Watts called out. 'What'll it be?'

Jack Lane's heart pounded in his chest. His mouth was sand dry. Sweat broke from every pore.

'You've got a deal, Mr Watts,' he called back.

Charlie Brady hung his head low, because he reckoned that this was the last time he would see his longtime friend Jack Lane alive.

The slither of a disturbed rattler in nearby rocks made Lane's mare even more edgy than she had already been. *I guess I'd better prepare my widow's weeds.* Martha Lane's bitter words came back to him, when he had arrived home to tell her that he had accepted Lucas Watts's offer. Reasoned argument had flown out through the window.

'Charlie Brady's promised to drop by every day while I'm gone,' he had said by way of comfort.

Martha had turned her back on him, and that was the way she had remained until he was out of sight. Then the tears she had kept in check flowed freely and she was beset with regret at not having relented from her cold-shoulder treatment, and was already grieving at being a widow.

Jack Lane was a good honest farmer. Ike Durrel was a born killer with gun know-how in spades. What other outcome could there be from such an uneven contest. Martha Lane could understand her husband's need to secure their future, of course. But, as a widow, what future would there be for her and the baby, orphaned before he was born.

Lane fretted that Ben Clark, drunk, would

spread the story of the man looking for Durrel. Along the way he had checked his backtrail several times and saw no sign of pursuit. Of course, that did not mean that he was not being followed. Because the kind of *hombre* who would dog his tail would probably be skilled in the ways of staying out of sight until he was good and ready to show himself, while he was not skilled in reading sign at all.

Indians, too, had the exact same skill of staying out of sight. A couple of times he thought he had felt eyes on him. But that might be just a figment of his overworked imagination. And Jack Lane, knowing more about seed and seasons than guns and tracking, was only too conscious of how ill-equipped he was for the task he had taken on.

Once the mare became resigned to going on Lane had had the good sense to let the horse find its own way down the shale track from the rise from which he had made the latest check on his backtrail. A time, on the steep track, the mare's hind legs almost went from under her and he was lucky to stay in the saddle. That was another lesson he was learning fast. He was a rank amateur in horsemanship when it came to riding the twistingly deceptive desert terrain.

All in all, as he rode deeper into the canyon, Jack Lane counted the dangers stacked against him, any one of which could prove fatal. Indians.

Terrain. Desert heat. Ike Durrel and any others of his kind he might have to tangle with.

He'd need luck by the ton if he was to ever see Martha again.

CHAPTER FOUR

Not far into the canyon the breeze, hot though it was, died – blocked out by the high canyon walls off which wave after wave of scorching heat shimmered, turning the canyon to a cauldron which would make hell fire cool. Lane's eyes constantly scanned the top of the canyon and its high reaches where the Apaches liked to lurk. However, looking skywards made him vulnerable to threats and dangers from lower down. Any boulder, tumble of rocks or ridge could hide an enemy of the two or four-legged kind. Dividing his attention could be his undoing. The sandy soil of the track also held dangers. It shifted easily and unexpectedly, sometimes collapsing into holes of which there was no hint until they opened up. It would be easy for the mare to break a leg in such an unexpected trap. Snakebite, too, could disable the horse, leaving him high and dry and as good as dead.

A vulture circled overhead, quickly joined by another, and soon after by a third and a fourth. Were they just curious? Or maybe hopeful? From their lofty height, did they know something he was not yet aware of?

Jack Lane smelled the stench before, coming round a bend, he came up short on seeing the rotting corpse of a man sitting against a boulder as if he had paused to grub or rest. He had, in the main, been picked clean by the buzzards. Tendrils of shrivelled brain matter dangled from empty eyesockets through which long and sharp beaks had explored. He was no sawbones, but Lane reckoned that the deep purple of his face and lips suggested that the man had died of a heart attack, a not uncommon occurrence in the hellishly hot country.

The empty water canteen near the dead man made Jack Lane acutely conscious of the precious water in his canteen, but he fought his thirst. He had filled two canteens before he left Huntley, but he had partaken fairly liberally from one of the canteens until now the remaining water sloshed hollowly in it. The map Ben Clark had drawn for him had already proved incorrect in that a water hole he had marked had not been there. He supposed that in the desert water holes probably

came and went in the constantly shifting land-
scape. However, the error was worrying. And one
mistake raised the question of how many more
errors there might be in the map? He did not
doubt Clark's sincerity, but rotgut had a way of soft-
ening a man's brain until delusion often wore the
cloak of certainty. Or, in fairness to Ben Clark, the
mistake might be down to his own inexperience as
a map reader.

'Hope I have better luck than you, friend,' Jack
Lane told the corpse.

As he was about to ride on, Lane spotted the
edge of what he reckoned was a saddlebag wedged
between a couple of boulders on higher ground
behind where the dead man lay. He nudged the
mare up the rise of ground, dismounted, and
retrieved the saddlebag. The dead man must have
hidden the bag before misfortune had befallen
him. He undid the straps of the bulging saddlebag, and when he flipped it open he was dumb-
founded. The saddlebag was packed with dollar
bills of various denominations, the sum of which
must have amounted to many thousands of
dollars. The bills were in bundles and bearing the
wrap of the Hoddsville Bank. In a blink, Lane
made the connection with the recent robbery of
the bank with one Samuel Connell, the bank-
teller who went missing the same time as the
bank's money. Recalling the story in the newspa-

per, Connell had been twenty years working for the bank and enjoyed the absolute trust of the bank owners, to the point where he had been issued with a key to the vault. One night, soon after being placed in such a trustworthy position, Samuel Connell had let himself into the bank, and when the bank opened for business the next morning all that had been left in the vault was petty cash.

Flabbergasted, Jack Lane sat on the stony ground, flicking the bundles of dollar bills. Samuel Connell had handed him a fortune and a mountain of temptation. He could now forget about Ike Durrel. No one would know where the Hoddsville Bank loot had got to. And if he spent it sparingly, growing prosperous over time, folk would think that his enhanced lifestyle was as a result of his shrewd business acumen.

In a gleeful mood, Jack Lane was in the saddle and ready to hightail it when he realized that he could not do it. Not because of any guilt about purloining what already had been purloined; his guilt sprang from abandoning his search for Emily Watts. Durrel might already have sold Emily across the border to a Mex whorehouse, or as a concubine to a rich Mexican. Or she might be suffering Durrel's foul attentions. The other possibility was that she was already dead. Whatever, as a half-decent human being, he had a duty to find her and get her back to her pa. Or at least word of her fate.

That left Jack Lane with a pickle of a dilemma. If he took the money with him and got waylayed, he'd lose every dime of his good fortune. And if he hid it, someone might stumble on it the way he had. Or, not knowing the topography of the terrain, if he stashed it he might never again find it. That particular possibility broke a cold sweat on Lane.

'Now what the heck am I going to do with this loot, horse?' he asked the mare. The mare snorted. 'Now ain't it a darn pity I can't understand horse-talk,' he said.

Lane pondered feverishly for another couple of minutes before an idea took hold. He went and moved the corpse aside, dug a hole under it, placed the saddlebag in the hole, filled it in, and returned the dead man to the same spot he had been occupying, feeling guilty that he had not buried him, but reasoning that it made no difference to the dead man. Then he went and searched until he found a sliver of rock with a point as sharp as a nib. Returning to the corpse, on the boulder against which the dead man rested, he scraped in bold letters:

BEWARE. DIED OF FEVER.

Jack Lane stepped back and studied his handiwork for dramatic effect, and was pleased with what he saw. The chilling warning, fever being the scurge every man feared (even though the man was long gone), no one would want to risk catching the pestilence by going anywhere near him. And furthermore, Lane figured that he could not have found a better marker to the Hoddsville Bank stash.

Pleased with his scheme for hiding the loot, Jack Lane's eyes took in his surroundings inch by careful inch, until he was as satisfied as he could be that he was alone. Then he mounted up and rode away, careful from there on to note any distinctive landmark on the trail he travelled which would guide him back to where his unexpected windfall was buried. That was, of course, he glumly contemplated, if he was coming back.

Well into the canyon, his nerves jangling as the trail got narrower and narrower, bringing the rocky slopes nearer every second, Lane's concerns grew. Any lurker on the sweeps of shale and rock either side of the trail would be near impossible to spot until it was too late to do anything to avoid a bushwhacking. His only hope was that in the intense silence of the canyon, any movement by a would-be waylayer would be signalled in good time. Because it would be near impossible for anyone to stir without causing a disturbance in the sandy shale. And the loosening of a pebble would be heard in the stillness. However, there was one possible enemy to which that rule did not apply.

Apaches.

They could move ghostlike through terrain where the most agile and light-footed whiteman could not. The mare, however, would be a guide to possible trouble. At the moment the horse was sauntering, unconcerned, as if ambling across a soft meadow. Any change in the mare's mood, even the smallest one, Jack Lane was ready to note.

As the walls of the canyon closed in even further still, the sunlight was squeezed into a narrow shaft like a glinting dagger. Its confined beam showed less and less of the terrain ahead, allowing for pools of shadow to form; dangerous shaded spots that could hold a threat unseen until it was too late to act.

The canyon became breathless, its air squeezed by its walls and forced to a furnace heat.

'There ain't no other way to Ned Durrel's place, unless you've got most of a week to spare through the hills to come at the valley from its northern side. And if you do that, it'll mean riding in over flat country without cover,' Ben Clark had told him, and had added, 'Besides, you're a greenhorn in this neck of the woods, and you'd likely run into more trouble in the hills than the desert.'

Lane had reminded Clark that he was as much of a greenhorn taking the route he had mapped out for him.

'The thing with the hills, unless you can sniff trouble in the air long before it shows itself, is that you don't see trouble 'til it bites you in the ass,' Clark said. 'And by then, it's way too late to do anything about it.'

Glancing around him now, Jack Lane was at a loss to appreciate Clark's point of view. Because, as far as he could see, trouble could bite him in the ass in the terrain he was riding through as fast as it would in the hills. He began to fret that Ben Clark had seen a greenhorn and made even a bigger greenhorn of him. With the demons riding on Clark's back, a bottle of rotgut could be the price of his very soul, let alone sending a stranger on a wild-goose chase.

He took Clark's map from his pocket and checked again for anything he might have missed. But, as far as he could fathom, he had not seen any landmarks that Clark had noted on the map. There were two possibilities, Lane glumly concluded. Either he had strayed or Clark, seeing a free bottle, had drawn a map that was a figment of his befuddled brain.

Jack Lane's hopes were sinking faster than Ben

Clark sank whiskey when, almost at the end of the canyon, he saw a jutting rockface that Clark had described as looking like a hooked nose and, recalling Clark's description of the terrain beyond, Lane reckoned that the drunk had described perfectly its contours. 'Must mean that Clark knows what he's talking about, don't it?' Lane asked the mare, who snorted.

Uplifted, Jack Lane urged the mare forward, anxious to be clear of the canyon and its breath-cloying airlessness. The mare not being in the flush of youth, he put her lack-lustre response down to tiredness. When two men emerged from either side of the trail to block his path, Jack Lane saw that he had ridden headlong into trouble – big trouble.

The men brandished cocked sixguns.

'Hold it right there, friend,' the taller of the two ordered Lane.

'Unless you want to feel hot lead in your belly,' the second man warned.

Jack Lane brought the mare up short, cursing that he had not correctly interpreted her sluggishness as disinclination, rather than the vagaries of long-toothedness.

'Sensible fella,' the taller man said.

'Ain't that a real shame, Henry,' the second man said. 'I had me a hankerin' to kill someone.'

The mare backed off, excited by the trophies

hanging on belts round the men's waists – Indian scalps.

Scalp-hunters!

CHAPTER FIVE

'What can I do you for, gents?' Lane enquired of the obviously murderous duo, the bloody evidence of their evil characters hanging from their belts. He had couched his question in a way that made it seem, he hoped, that their appearance did not unduly trouble him. However, their sniggering response quickly told him that his show of nonchalance had not fooled them.

'*What can I do for you gents?*' the taller one mocked Lane, much to the amusement of his sidekick, who laughed as if he had heard the world's best joke. 'Well, I'll tell ya what ya can do for Henry and me, mister. You can climb down from that nag and hand it over to us. Ya see, me and Henry had to run our nags into the ground to stay ahead of some 'Paches who kinda don't like us any. Now ain't that just lousy luck.'

He chuckled meanly.

'Leastways, 'tis for you, mister.'

Jack Lane, figuring that the toerags could kill him anyway, just for the fun of seeing him die, decided that he might as well play the only ace in his deck.

'Now fellas,' he drawled. 'Before you take to horse-thieving, I reckon I should tell you something that might change your minds, and prevent you acting in a rash and hasty manner.'

'Is he talkin' American, Larry?' the man called Henry wondered.

'Don't rightly know, Henry,' Larry said. 'But whatever lingo he's spoutin', I figure it's comin' right outta his rear end.' Henry laughed as if he had heard the world's second-best joke. Larry drew a Colt .45 and thumbed back the hammer. 'Now, mister, if you ain't outta that saddle pronto I'll put a bullet right 'tween your eyes.'

'Now that's American, Larry,' Henry chuckled, slapping his knee and dancing about like the town idiot.

'Let me get straight to the point, Larry,' Lane said.

'Aw shit, Larry,' Henry swore. 'Just plug the bastard and be done with it!'

The sudden edginess in Henry made Lane think that he was a better actor than he had thought he was.

'Shush,' Larry said impatiently. 'Let the man have his speak.' Henry obviously thought Larry had taken leave of his senses, and stated as much. 'A man 'bout to die deserves his final words, Henry,' Larry said.

Disgruntled, Henry said, 'Well, get on with it, friend.' He patted the scalps on his belt. 'Ain't 'xactly the right place to be hangin' round with these. 'Paches get mighty upset if you part them from their hair, especially their womenfolks' hair.'

He snorted.

'Ain't got no sense of humour, 'Paches.'

'I'm waitin' for you to say what you've got to say, mister,' the man called Larry growled.

'OK,' Jack Lane said, leaning back in his saddle, striking a pose of ease. 'You fellas ever heard of Ike Durrel?'

Henry and Larry exchanged alarmed glances.

'I can see that you boys have. And I can also see that you'd prefer to match wits any day with Apaches than Ike.'

'You, ah, know Ike Durrel?' Henry managed to ask, his voice now rasping as the spittle in his mouth dried up.

Jack Lane crossed his fingers.

'Like so,' he said. 'Now, I can assure you fellas that if I told Ike what happened just now, he'd be mighty upset. And Ike, upset. . . .' Lane shook his head.

Larry thumbed back the hammer of the Colt and dropped the pistol into its holster as if it was a hot coal.

'Real sensible, Larry,' Lane crowed.

'We didn't mean no harm, friend,' Larry said. 'Me and Henry was just foolin' round, ya understand.'

'Yeah,' Henry said, whiningly. 'Like Larry said, we was just horsin' round.'

'That's good to know,' Lane said. 'Because if I had to tell Ike that you boys tried to waylay me, well, he'd be hopping mad and would come looking for you gents.'

Henry and Larry came as close to leaning on each other for support as made no difference.

'You be sure to tell Ike that we send him our best,' Henry said, almost choking for want of breath.

'Tell you what, fellas,' Lane said, now relishing the role he was playing. 'Let's forget we ever crossed paths, huh?'

'Yeah,' the scalp-hunters chimed in unison. 'Thank ya, mister. Thank ya kindly.'

Lane rode on.

'Be seeing you gents around,' he called back over his shoulder, resisting the urge to look back, realizing that it might dawn on Henry and Larry that a dead friend of Ike Durrel would not be able to tell him anything. But if he turned they might see the sweat flowing through every pore and cotton on to the fact that they had been hoodwinked. It was a gamble that he'd rather not have to make. And the question uppermost in Jack Lane's mind, as he distanced himself from the scalphunters was, did they have the brains to reach the conclusion he had.

'Heh, mister . . .' Jack Lane sat his saddle rigid. He swung round slowly to face Henry. 'Didn't catch your name?'

'Jack Lane.' Lane said, and rode on again.

'Nice knowin' ya, Jack,' Larry called.

'Nice knowing you, Larry,' Lane replied, picking up his pace but not too much, not wanting to seem too anxious to put ground between them.

Larry scratched his head. 'Who's Jack Lane, Henry?'

'Don't know for shit, Larry,' Henry said, scratching his chin stubble, puzzled. 'Never heard of no Jack Lane.'

'Kinda in a hurry, of a sudden, ain't he?' Larry observed, as Lane quickened his pace.

Henry's eyes narrowed. 'Larry,' he said, grimly. 'I reckon that fella Lane don't know Ike Durrel from Adam.'

He drew his .45 and began shooting. Larry joined in, until they both emptied their chambers in useless leadslinging, as Lane had gone too far for their handguns to be effective.

'He really suckered ya, didn't he,' Larry accused Henry.

'If I ever see that bastard again,' Henry raged. 'I'll kill him!'

'Aw, shuddup!' Larry ranted.

Out of sight, Jack Lane drew rein to breathe deeply. 'That, horse,' he groaned, 'was a call closer than I liked.'

His relief was brief. His would-be killers were scalp-hunters, and the scalps on their belts were recently taken. That meant that there were a lot of riled-up Apaches looking for revenge. And Lane figured that they would not be too particular about whose hair they took, provided the face below it was white.

When it came to dregs, scalp-hunters were the scum at the bottom of the barrel. There was only one species of lowlife worse, and that was the men who paid the scalp-hunters for their grisly souvenirs. Without them the gruesome business would not exist. He had heard that up to twenty dollars was the going rate for an Indian scalp.

'You veer north about a mile out of the canyon,' Ben Clark's words came winging back to Jack Lane. 'Half a day's ride in a straight line from there you'll come to the ruins of an old mission called O'Flaherty's Mistake, that's 'cause the Capuchin missioner who reckoned that he could bring the word of his god to the Apache was a fella called Michael John O'Flaherty from County Cork. And he almost did, too,' Clark had said with a shining pride in his liquor-washed-out eyes, 'until two no-good bastards masquerading as priests from the mission raped and scalped six Apache women.'

Henry and Larry? Lane wondered.

'When the scalped women were found, one clutching a crucifix she had torn from one of the scalp-hunters, the kind the priests at the mission wore, a raiding party killed everyone at the mission. Michael John O'Flaherty they tortured for most of a week before he died.

'There's a good well at the mission. Flaherty came from Irish farming stock and knew how to find and keep good water. You can rest there and fill your canteens. 'Cause by then the easy part of your journey will be over.'

Jack Lane sighed.

'The easy part will be over soon, horse, you hear,' he groaned. The mare lowered her head, as if she understood every word he had said, and also their ridiculousness. He urged the mare forward. 'Next stop O'Flaherty's Mistake,' he said.

The mare's response was listless, and Jack Lane prayed that between where he was and the mission, the mare would not be called upon for pace.

CHAPTER SIX

Four gruelling hours later, the sun was sliding down the horizon when, from a rise up which he had ridden, Lane saw on a flat, smooth basin of land O'Flaherty's Mistake. Jack Lane reckoned that it was only a man of faith who would have chosen the site to build his mission, because the higher ground on all sides left the mission vulnerable to attack. Lane held back until nightfall before riding in, time during which he continually scanned the ruined mission for any sign of life. At last, as satisfied as he could be that he would not have company, Lane rode down from the ridge from which he had been watching, ready at the slightest hint of trouble in waiting to turn tail.

As he drew near to the mission Jack Lane had a sense of eyes on him. Or was that his imagination acting up? The dusk was full of shadows: odd ghostly shapes cast up by the grey light. There were already pools of shadow from which danger could spring. It was a place of eerie, unsettling stillness; a quietude made all the more haunting by the sudden cessation of a breeze that had been blowing, leaving the evening completely still. Lane was beginning to think that he had taken the wrong decision to wait until dusk to ride in. As he drew nearer still he could see the shapes of buildings behind the mission walls, most of which seemed to be tumbling in on themselves. But their decrepitude was all the more reason for concern: the buildings would provide a hundred hidey-holes from where an ambush might come.

Jack Lane's thoughts turned to the scalp-hunters he had hoodwinked. He told himself that he need not fear for their presence. He had left them horseless and hours behind him. But however he reasoned with himself, he could not get rid of the niggling idea that they might have made up ground. Henry and Larry had to be owl-wise and cunning to have survived in the hostile country they practised their evil trade in. It was a land in which the Grim Reaper roamed free, and was seldom disappointed. Apaches would be just one worry for them. But the men who rode the trails through the desert were men shunned by society and for good reason; they were outcasts from where decent folk lived because of the evils they perpetrated. The scalp-hunters might have got horses from fellow-scalpers or from some other equally vile source. A lot of men travelling the outlaws' trails had a spare horse in tow so that if needs be they could change mounts and have a fresh horse for the chase or the escape. Of necessity, there was a camaraderie between the men of like kind and mind. Because what was good fortune today could be bad luck tomorrow, and they would need help in turn.

Close to the mission entrance Jack Lane drew rein and gave over his full attention to listening to the silence in the hope that if there was something to be heard, he'd hear it in good time. But there was nothing to be heard except the breeze which had blown up again, whistling through the abandoned mission.

As he entered the mission night came suddenly, the way it did in the desert. 'Hello, the mission,' he called out. He got no response. Either there was no one there, or, if there was, that body did not feel like making his presence known. And not making their presence known probably meant that any lurker or lurkers were far from friendly or honourable. Lane's greeting echoed back hollowly. The mare shifted uneasily, spooked, Jack Lane hoped, by his disembodied voice and not by any malign threat.

He checked out the tumbledown buildings, and to his relief found them devoid of another soul except perhaps for the ghost of O'Flaherty.

Satisfied, he set up camp in the ruin of the old mission church. He gathered some kindling and started a fire to prepare a meagre meal from meagre rations. So far he had been almost a month looking for Ike Durrel, a couple of times coming close to catching him up. Only by three days in Huntley.

'Darn lucky you did, too,' had been Ben Clark's opinion, and he had added, 'If you take my advice, you'll turn for home and leave Durrel be.'

'He's got a woman he took hostage in a bank raid in a burg called Arrow Bend,' Lane told Clark. 'I've promised her pa that I'll do my best to get her back.'

Clark had looked at him through hazy eyes.

'Ain't as upstanding and rosy as that though, is it?' observed the former marshal of Huntley, shrewdly. 'Paying a bounty, is he, her pa?'

'Bounty? Not in my understanding of a bounty,' Lane had defended himself tersely. 'Lucas Watts is a banker. He'll wipe out what's due on my farm, and provide me with enough to tide me over until matters improve.'

'Bounty!' Clark had stated. 'No matter what fancy name or reason you give it, it's bounty.' His contempt for bounty hunters was etched in every line of his liquor-ravaged face. 'I ain't exactly parlour company myself. But compared to a bounty hunter, I reckon I'm of blue-blood stock, mister.'

Lane had argued hotly that his motivation to rescue Emily Watts was a noble one.

'Would you have hunted Durrel down if there was no bounty on offer?' Ben Clark had questioned Jack Lane with a fierceness that was principle-driven rather than whiskey-fuelled. 'The answer is simple, ain't it?' The former marshal had spat contemptuously when Lane could not hold his accusing gaze. 'Like, I said, bounty!'

Now, sitting by the fire watching the shadows dancing on the wall, Jack Lane was happy that his search for Ike Durrel was for more than to collect Lucas Watts' money. Because, had that been his only purpose, he would have ended his search and hightailed it when he had found the loot from the Hoddsville Bank. Even if he had not kept the money and had collected the reward, he'd still have had more than what Lucas Watts was paying him.

A shadow that had not previously been on the wall brought an instant tension to his spine. Because, unless the reflection from the fire was playing cruel tricks on him, the long shape was holding a sixgun. His hand dropped to his pistol.

'Ease it out slowly, mister,' the man said in a snarling voice he had heard before in the saloon in Huntley.

It was the voice of Ed Rekton.

'Don't look such a big man now, do he, Ed?' Al Baker said.

He had been the fool of all fools. Tangling with
the Rektons and their sidekick cousin Al Baker,
had been the kind of dumb thing that would probably send him winging skywards now. Jack Lane
turned slowly. There was only Ed Rekton and
Baker behind him. Where were Dan and Luke
Rekton? Lane reckoned that the outfit had split up
to cover more ground in their hunt for the man
they knew as Frank Stiller.

'How d'ya reckon we should kill him, Ed?' Baker
asked, his eyes already glowing with the pleasure to
come.

'Slow,' Rekton said. He settled poison-filled eyes
on Lane. 'Real slow.'

'I figure we should stake the bastard out and
peel his skin off inch by inch,' Baker said. 'Like the
'Paches do.'

Ed Rekton's high-pitched laughter chilled Jack
Lane's blood.

'That's a real good idea, Al,' he agreed. 'Maybe
we'll cut him just enough. Bleed him to attract the
buzzards or some four-legged critter to feast on
him while he's still alive.'

Warming to the cruelty of Rekton's scheme, Al
Baker proposed another demise. 'Remember what
that Mex bastard Sancho used to do. That trick
with the snake.'

Ed Rekton slapped his knee in delight.

'Yeah,' he said, obviously having settled for his

sidekick's suggestion. 'Real interestin', sittin' and watchin'.' Rekton was already breathless at the prospect.

'Only one thing.' Baker, suddenly jittery, looked like he regretted having voiced the idea. 'We gotta wait 'til the sun is high for that trick to work.'

'We ain't in no hurry,' Rekton barked.

'Take it easy, Ed,' Baker counselled. 'No need to get all mean. All I been doin' is thinkin' 'bout them scalped 'Pache women we found in that gully aways back. Now, 'Paches don't scalp each other. That means that there's scalp-hunters in the neighbourhood.'

Ed Rekton now shared in his cousin's unease.

'Likely when them savages find their women, there'll be 'Paches lookin' for them scalp-hunters.'

'But we ain't them scalp-hunters,' Rekton reasoned.

'You figure that bloodthirsty riled up 'Paches are goin' to be polite enough to ask a whiteman in Indian country questions! Bein' here in the first place is enough for them bastards to skin a whiteman alive. Lord knows what they'll get up to after they've found their women with their skirts hitched up, legs apart and hairless.'

Ed Rekton swallowed hard.

'Mebbe we should just cut this bastard's throat and make tracks outta Indian country while we still gotta chance,' Rekton said.

'Prob'ly the sensible thing to do, Ed.'

'Damn!' Rekton swore, angry that he had to forego Lane's torture. His hand slapped aside the knife which Baker was handing him. 'There'll be no Indians on the prowl in the dark. Let's wait 'til mornin'. See what it brings.'

' 'Paches, Ed,' Al Baker said breathlessly. 'Lookin' to add our scalps to their tally.'

'Don't make no diffrence what we do,' Rekton proclaimed. 'If we stay put, the savages might come a-callin' sure enough. But if we ride out, come mornin' we could be eye to eye with them, too.'

'Makes no sense to stay put, in my book,' Baker argued, fear making him defiant.

Defiance was something Ed Rekton was not used to, or liked. 'We wait 'til mornin', and that's an end of it, Al,' he declared.

Jack Lane looked on, pleased. A falling out between the outlaws could only be helpful to him. So he decided to stoke the angst that had built up between Rekton and his saddle partner. 'He's right, Rekton. If the Apaches will come here, you'll be sitting targets. Now if you were on horseback, you could at least give them a run. And who knows, maybe outrun them?'

'Shuddup!' Rekton bellowed, and swung a boot to Lane's ribs that had him gagging. 'Ain't no one asked ya for no opinion.'

'He's right,' Baker said, even bolder now.

'Can't ya see what he's up to, Al?' Rekton growled. 'Stiller figures that us fightin' with each other, he'll have a chance to save his flea-bitten hide.' Though not the brightest wick in the West, Baker had arrived at the same conclusion, but he did not care a fig. All he wanted was to get in the saddle and hightail it. When Al Baker did not readily agree, Ed Rekton's hand dropped to the butt of his sixgun. 'And I'd look mighty unkindly on a partner runnin' out on me,' he added menacingly.

Al Baker thought about continuing with his challenge but, uncertain as to whether he could outdraw Rekton (some said he could, and some said he could not), he reckond that backing off was the wiser thing to do.

'We stay 'til mornin'!' said Rekton, with finality.

CHAPTER SEVEN

The moon was riding high in the sky when Jack Lane eventually cut through the last couple of threads of the rawhide binding his hands behind his back. He felt the slash of the sharp edge of a stone poking out of the mission church wall which, over the previous hour, he had stealthily inched towards. The pain from the slash raced up his arm and, it being his right hand, he hoped that he had not cut a nerve or tendon that would disable his gunhand, not that he had a gun any more. But there might be a possibility of getting hold of one, if his plan worked as he hoped it would.

He settled his position against the wall and, as if waking from sleep, groaned. Al Baker, whose watch it was, woke from a fitful sleep at the sound of Lane's moaning.

'It's the circulation in my hands,' Lane said. 'It's stopped.'

'So?' Baker growled.

'So I'm getting a pain in my chest that's getting worse all the time. A heart attack will rob Rekton of the pleasure of watching me die. And if that happens, he'll take it out of your hide, I reckon.'

'Horseshit! You don't get a heart attack from havin' your hands tied behind your back, Stiller.'

'Do you want to take that chance?' Rekton's sidekick looked to where the outlaw was bundled up under his blanket in a nook at the other side of the church, seemingly sleeping peacefully under a frameless window. 'He'll be mad as hell, if I become a harp player before he decides that I should.'

Making up his mind, Baker came over to where Jack Lane was.

'Turn round.'

Lane made a show of stiffness and grimaced as he moved.

'Give me a hand. I'm crippled fairly badly,' he complained.

'You want that knot loosed, you'll turn yourself,' Baker said.

Jack Lane made another show of trying to turn and groaned.

'Shuddup!' Baker ordered, through lips that were a mere slit, his glance shooting back to where Rekton was sleeping. Satisfied that Rekton had not been disturbed, he leaned forward to help Lane turn round, just as Lane had wanted him to do.

Jack Lane brought his knee up into the outlaw's groin. Baker doubled over, his face a mask of pain. Lane followed through with a boot that caught Baker on the side of the head. The outlaw, unbalanced and prey to a telling blow from Lane, took the full punishment of the blow. However, instinct told Lane that all was not right. The sound of a sixgun being cocked, from a place he had never expected, finished Lane's bid for freedom.

'Reckoned that a smart fella like you might have a trick or two up your sleeve, Stiller. Figured you'd try to hoodwink Al, and that he'd prob'ly be suckered because he ain't too bright. So I slipped out that window I was lying under and waited for you to make your move.'

Rekton had the gait of a peacock.

'And lucky I did, too.'

'Said he was havin' a heart attack, Ed,' was Baker's limp defence; a defence Rekton scoffed at.

'I should kill you, Al,' Rekton ranted. 'But,' Rekton's mood became expansive, 'I reckon every man is fooled sometime.'

'Let me kill him right now, Ed,' Baker snarled.

'No. It's only a couple of hours to sun-up. And it won't be long after that, that the sun will be strong enough for our little trick.'

'I'm goin' to enjoy watchin' you sweat, mister,' said Baker spitefully to Lane. 'And watch you go loco when that snake gets nearer and nearer.' He laughed insanely.

'Get some shut-eye, Al. I'll watch this slippery Dan 'til sun-up.'

As Baker walked to where his bedroll was, Lane said, 'Walks real good for a dead man, don't you think, Rekton.'

Al Baker came up short. 'What the hell're you gabbin' about, Stiller?'

'Go to bed, Al,' Rekton snarled.

'You think about it, Baker,' Lane said. 'How useful you'll be once I'm dead.'

'Shuddup!' Ed Rekton ordered Lane.

'Rekton would have killed you right now, if he didn't need your help with me.'

Rekton raked the barrel of his pistol across Jack Lane's right cheek, opening up a deep gash.

Al Baker's eyes glistened with suspicion. 'Ed and me are kin, Stiller.'

'You don't believe that horse manure, do you? Rekton snorted. 'Stiller's talkin' through his rear end, Al.'

'When I'm dead, you're dead too, Baker,' Lane said, and got Ed Rekton's boot in his ribs as a punishment.

'I told you to shuddup, Stiller!' Rekton barked. 'One more word and I'll empty this sixgun in you.' He swung round on Baker. 'You still here!'

Thoughtful of mood, Al Baker continued on to where his bedroll was.

Jack Lane reckoned that he had sown the seeds of doubt in Al Baker's mind. However, his strategy was doubled-edged. Because by fostering suspicion in Baker, he had also put Ed Rekton on guard and, consequently, the outlaw would be ready to make his move if Baker showed any signs of rebellion.

It would be a long and edgy couple of hours to sun-up, during which Jack Lane would have a lot to ponder on, like never seeing his wife again or his son or daughter. It looked like Charlie Brady was right.

It had been a loco idea to go after Ike Durrel.

Sun-up came much too quickly.

CHAPTER EIGHT

'Time for fun and games, Stiller,' Rekton declared, with pagan relish. 'Get him on his feet, Al.'

Baker complied readily, eager to compensate for his earlier blunder. When he bent down to haul Lane to his feet, Lane whispered, in a last throw of the dice, 'Rekton will kill you for sure, Baker.'

'No he won't,' Baker said. 'Me and Ed's been saddle pards for ten years. That counts for somethin'.'

'Not with Rekton, it won't,' Lane said. 'You're a fool, Baker.'

'It's you're the fool, Stiller,' Baker spat. 'You're the one trussed up and ready for killin'.'

'What're you pair gabbin' about?' Rekton enquired suspiciously.

'Nothin',' Al Baker answered hurriedly, his nerves all a jangle.

'Stake him out,' Rekton ordered Baker. He ran a finger round inside his collar. 'It's already got the feel of a real hot day.'

Outside, Baker drove four stakes into the ground while Rekton held Lane under threat of his sixgun. Stakes driven, Rekton ordered, 'Tie him down, Al.' Al Baker's eagerness to please Rekton was all the greater, and he beavered away to complete the task Rekton had set him. Ed Rekton gloatingly circled the helpless Lane. 'Nice job, Al,' he complimented his sidekick. The ground under Jack Lane was already scorching his back and with the sun shooting upwards, before long, he reckoned, he would be willing to exchange hell for what he had. 'You know what to do,' Rekton told Baker. When Baker drove a thin pliable stick into the ground behind his head and tied a string of rawhide to it, Lane wondered what torture they had in mind, but he did not have to wonder for long. 'Now go charm a rattler, Al.' It became immediately clear to Lane what Rekton had in mind, and his blood chilled to zero. 'Al's got this way with rattlers, Stiller,' Rekton explained. 'He can look one in the eye and hypno- tize the critter.'

'Learned the trick from a Comanche,' Al Baker boasted.

'It's the darnest thing,' Ed Rekton said, shaking his head in wonder.

'Be back in no time at all.' Baker hurried away.

'Strange thing about Al,' Rekton said. 'I seen

him on his belly eye-to-eye with a rattler, talkin' to him like he'd talk to you or me. Kinda makes me wonder what he's made up of inside.'

'The exact same rottenness as you,' Lane said.

'You've got a real smart mouth, Stiller.' Rekton glowered. 'Let's see how smart you'll be with a rattler spittin' in your eye.'

In no time at all, Baker was back, holding a rattler that was as tame as a fireside cat. He tied the rattlesnake by the tail to the string of rawhide. The weight of the snake looped the thin flexible stick over him. Lane watched the snake, both mesmerized and terrified by its hypnotizing evil look. 'Now all we need is some animal fat to grease the rawhide.' Baker went to his saddlebag and came back with strips of bacon, the fat from which he applied liberally to the string of rawhide. The heat of the sun melted the fat as he rubbed it in. Satisfied, he said, 'Now step back, Ed. When I wake this critter up, he'll be as mad as hell for havin' been fooled.' Al Baker made a low crooning sound. The snake wriggled sluggishly. 'That's my beauty,' he coaxed the reptile, gently rubbing the rattler's head. He took his crooning to a higher pitch and the rattlesnake came awake from the trance Baker had put it into. And, as he had predicted, the rattler was mad as hell. Its ugly head darted about until, slowly, its evil eyes came to concentrate on Lane.

'Now, slowly that strip of rawhide will heat, then it will smoulder, and then it will burn.' Ed Rekton explained, feverishly. 'When it burns through, that rattler will fall right on your face, Stiller.' Ed Rekton sat on the ground to watch, his eyes every inch as evil as the rattler's. He laughed. 'Of course you'll prob'ly die of fright long before that.'

'He'll get riled more and more every second,' Baker said, sharing in Rekton's amusement.

'Hot, ain't it,' Rekton said, looking to the ball of fire in the sky. He looked at the whirls of white smoke coming from the greased rawhide, becoming tinged with darker smoke. 'Shouldn't have long to wait now.'

'This is goin' to be good fun, Ed,' Al Baker said, sitting on to the ground alongside Rekton.

'Sure is,' Rekton said. 'Only you ain't goin' to be 'round to see the end.' Al Baker felt the prod of Rekton's sixgun in his side. 'You ain't no more use, Al. You're plain stupid, ya see.' Ed Rekton squeezed the trigger. Rekton was clever. Baker's body flesh muffled the sound of the gun. 'We wouldn't want them 'Paches to hear, now would we, Al.' As Baker toppled against Rekton, he shoved him contemptuously aside.

Jack Lane was not in a position to take any plaudits for his astuteness in reading Rekton's intentions correctly. He was much too busy watching the rawhide start to smoulder. The rattler wriggled excitedly, its evil brain sensing pleasures to come soon.

'Ya know, I figure he ain't half mad enough yet, Stiller,' Rekton said.

To rile the snake further, Rekton took to teasing the rattler with a long stick. The smoke from the string of rawhide got blacker still, and Jack Lane saw a couple of dazzling sparks flash along it. There could only be, at the most he reckoned, another minute before the rawhide began to burn, and only seconds after that before it burned through and the rattlesnake dropped on him.

Buzzards hovered in a deathwatch. Some vultures, sensing Jack Lane's utter helplessness, were unable to wait and swooped. And if Ed Rekton had chosen not to scatter them, they would have struck before the rattler delivered up dead meat.

'You'll get your feast soon, buzzards,' Rekton shouted. 'But not before I wring every last second of pleasure from seeing this bastard turn to jelly afore my eyes.'

Giving the rattler another poke of his long stick, Ed Rekton chuckled, 'Any second now, Stiller. Ain't as smart-mouthed now as you were back in that saloon in Huntley, are ya?'

Jack Lane was a surprised and much relieved

man when a rifle shot shredded the rattler, dumping bloodied bits of the foul creature on Lane's face. Surprised as Jack Lane had been, Ed Rekton was utterly stunned. He sprang to his feet, his eyes feverishly searching for the shooter. A puff of smoke from the church tower told Rekton where he was, but it was information that came way too late. The outlaw dropped to his knees, curiously looking at the hole in his chest. A second bullet took the top of his head off.

Whoever the shooter in the bell tower of the church was, a man would pose no difficulty for him when he had dispatched a wriggling rattlesnake.

'Hello the tower!' Lane joyously hailed the shooter, before a dark and forbidding thought tempered his delight. He had assumed that the shooter was a friend, but that might not be so. Rekton's killer might have something else in mind, other than saving his life. Indeed, perhaps the shooter had saved him only to inflict other tortures on him. Rekton might have been killed because he was armed and free to act and had therefore been a danger to be eliminated. Jack Lane tried to stifle the dreaded thought coming to mind. Had he been mistaken for a scalp-hunter? Was the shooter an Indian? Could Indians shoot with such deadly accuracy? And a lone Apache? Didn't Indians hunt in packs? Or by a cruel twist of fate, had the scalp-hunters caught him up?

'Ain't you going to show yourself,' Lane called out.

When the shooter showed himself, for Jack Lane surprise was heaped on surprise.

CHAPTER NINE

'Howdy, friend,' Ben Clark greeted Lane. He disappeared from the tower and moments later came from the ruined church and crossed to where Jack Lane was staked out. 'Almost didn't make it to repay your debt of kindness to me. What the heck is your real name anyway?'

'Jack Lane.'

'Well, Jack,' Clark took a knife from his boot and cut the rawhide that bound him to the stakes. 'Sure nice to meet you again.'

Though stiff in every muscle, Lane sprang to his feet, marvelling at the clean-cut man who had been Huntley's town drunk only a couple of days previously.

'That was pretty impressive lead-slinging,' he congratulated Clark.

'I got lucky.'

Jack Lane dismissed the idea with a shake of his head. 'That shooting had nothing to do with luck. That was one hundred per cent skill.'

Ben Clark licked parched lips, and for a moment his eyes showed the pain of innards crying out for liquor. The hand holding his rifle trembled a little and he quickly changed the rifle to his other hand. Lane knew then that he had not witnessed a miracle, just a man who had temporally overcome his demons to help another man who had shown him kindness.

'Guess we'd better mount up and make tracks for Huntley,' Clark said, half-turning away to hide his shame as the shakes became more pronounced.

'I ain't going back to Huntley, Ben,' Lane said. 'I've got Ike Durrel to snare, and a young woman to rescue.'

Clark swung around, wide-eyed. 'I didn't just save your hide for you to throw it away again! And that's what you'll sure as hell do if you find Durrel or hang round these parts for long more.' Worry clouded his face. 'This is dangerous country any time. But right now the pot of hate is boiling over, Jack. Saw a war party an hour or so ago to the south of here.'

He pointed to hills to the west of the mission from where smoke was puffing.

'That smoke is telling of a couple of scalp-hunters that the Apaches want to get their hands on. And any whiteman they cross paths with in between will get the same treatment that those hair-robbing bastards will get when they catch up with them.'

'I won't go back on my word, Ben,' Lane proclaimed.

'Then you'll surely pay with your life for trying to keep it,' Clark predicted. 'Find Durrel and he'll kill you. Cross paths with the Indians – same thing. And, if you recall, the Rekton outfit had four men. There's only two here. That means that along with Durrel and the Apaches to worry about, you've also got Rekton's murdering brothers looking to settle a score with you. They obviously split up to cover more territory. So they could be waiting round the next bend, Jack.'

'It's a big country. Maybe we'll never cross paths.'

'Thing is, I've always found that even out here, when you don't want to run into someone, that's just when it darn well happens,' Clark said.

'I ain't giving up on Durell, Ben,' Jack Lane stated resolutely.

'Well, if you're so mule-headed about getting yourself killed, there's not a thing I can do to stop you,' Ben Clark declared. 'Might as well have stayed back in Huntley.' He stared Jack Lane down. Lane's stance remained resolute. Clark's sigh was a heavy one. 'Still got that map I drew for you?' Jack Lane produced the map from a pocket of his Levis. Clark took the map. 'I was pretty stewed when I drew this. Better check that everything is where it's supposed to be. The last thing you need is to put miles on to you that you don't need.'

'Appreciate your honesty,' Lane said. 'And your help, too, Ben.'

'Pity it will all be for naught.'

'Maybe luck will be with me.'

'In my experience, luck is a bitch who'll run out on you when you most need her, Jack.' A deep sadness showed briefly in Ben Clark's washed-out eyes 'I'm a prime example of that lady's fickleness, I reckon.'

'What pain put you on liquor, Ben?' Lane enquired kindly.

'My wife died in childbirth. I took a bottle or two to tide me over the rough patch. Pretty soon I found that I didn't have to have an excuse to get liquored up any more.'

Jack Lane's thoughts turned to Martha and his unborn child, and for the thousandth time he wondered if he had done the right thing in accepting Lucas Watts's proposition, even if it would, depending on a successful outcome, see him out of his financial bind.

'It's right,' Clark confirmed, after his brief

perusal of the map he had drawn. He pointed. 'Head in a straight line for those hills. You'll find Ned Durrel's place at the other side, at the end of a long narrow valley. Ned ain't as mean as Ike. Breaks and trades horses. Brews a little moonshine to keep the Indians sweet-natured to let him be. Some folk say that Ned even disapproves of his brother's shenanigans. However, he ain't ever closed his door to Ike when he needed a hidey-hole. Make no mistake, Jack. When push comes to shove, Ned Durrel will throw in his lot with Ike. Ned's real strong on kinship.

'Another thing you should know about. When Ned's in trouble, the Apaches come to help. Maybe, even getting the benefit of every miracle in the book, that'll make you see how high a mountain you'll have to climb to get out of this neck of the woods with that woman in tow. First you'll have to kill Ike and Ned Durrel, before you even tangle with the Apaches. Not to mention Dan and Luke Rekton.'

Jack Lane grinned wryly.

'You sure have a way of lifting a man's spirits, Ben,' he said.

'Just being blunt honest with you,' Clark responded, and then pleaded, 'Forget this madness, Jack. While there's still time.'

Jack Lane was honest enough to admit that he

was tempted to breaking-point.

'I can't break my word, Ben.'

'Well, if you make it, drop by Huntley on your way back.'

'That I'll surely do,' Lane promised. He watched Ben Clark ride away, now firmly in the grip of liquor fever. It would be a long and hard ride home. 'Good luck, friend,' he murmured.

Lane mounted up and rode in the opposite direction, towards the distant hills. Maybe a grave in the desert would be his sad lot, if anyone bothered to bury him. But maybe good fortune might favour him, too. Life was a damn melting-pot anyway.

His thoughts turned to the loot from the Hoddsville Bank that he had hidden. Would he ever see it again? Had he been the fool of all fools not to have headed back home with it? Even if he had returned the money to the bank, there could have been been a reward that might be even more handsome than the bounty Lucas Watts would pay him. A storm was creeping along the horizon, rolling up out of Mexico, its direction as yet undecided. He'd welcome the cooling balm of its rain, but not the storm's dangers of lightning and flash floods that could sweep a man away with the arrogant impunity that nature was capable of. 'Horse,' he groaned. 'You've got the dumbest critter in the West on board. You know that, don't you?' The mare snorted. 'No darn need to be so outspoken about it, horse,' he chuckled.

CHAPTER TEN

It was close to noon when the heat eventually
forced Jack Lane to take shelter under the overhang of a ridge that offered shade from the merci-
less sun. He ate a little jerky and sipped sparingly
from his canteen. The water was hot and tasted
weedy. He hoped that it had not gone foul. Bad
water had been the undoing of many a desert trav-
eller. Weakened, he would become prey to a host
of critters, four and two-legged and winged.
Vultures were constantly on the lookout for their
next meal. And sometimes, he'd heard tell, a
disabled man was, for the buzzards, a man as good
as dead. Even in the boiling desert heat Jack
Lane's blood ran cold when his imagination
conjured up an image of buzzards' beaks stripping
him of his flesh while he could still feel it being
ripped from his body.

Exhausted from a long, sleepless and worrisome
night and the torture that had followed, Jack

Lane's reserves of energy were at a low ebb and, unwittingly, he dozed. A spill of shale, like stones rattling in an empty bucket, jerked him from his uneasy slumber just as another handful of shale bounced off the boulders in front of him from the ridge above the overhang. The clomp of hoofs on the ridge had Lane sitting upright. Only one horse, that he could tell – shod. So his visitor or visitors were not Indians, but the threat to his safety was, in country abounding in cut-throats, no less. The ridge was not very high, however it offered a good vantage point to reconnoitre the flat and featureless terrain.

'Might as well be on the darn moon, Henry.'

Henry.

Wasn't that the monicker of one of the scalp-hunters whose clutches he had so fortunately escaped from? When Henry replied, Lane was left in no doubt. He instantly recognized the higher, almost whining pitch of the taller of the scalp-hunters.

'This nag is pretty tuckered out,' Henry said. 'Goin' to fold soon, I reckon.'

'That's 'cause you've been chasin' all over the place lookin' for that fella who made fools of us,' Larry complained. 'Instead of makin' tracks for Huntley and safety.'

'Didn't think it would take so long to hunt the bastard down, did I?' Henry groused. 'Still got me a feelin' he ain't far away.'

'Let's forget him and head for Huntley now, Henry,' Larry pleaded. 'With 'Paches on the prowl we've been lucky so far. But our luck can't hold out for ever.'

'Ain't you got any pride!' Henry exploded. 'Don't you want to make the bastard pay for his impudence.'

'I'd rather be a fool with hair than a fool without hair,' Larry argued. 'Sooner or later we'll cross paths with that *hombre* again, and then we can settle scores, Henry.'

There was a sullen silence before Henry conceded, 'Guess you're right, Larry.'

'Sure I am,' Larry said eagerly. 'Huntley, huh?'

'Yeah. Hope the nag holds out.' Jack Lane's relief was immense. Then the mare snuffled. 'Wait! Thought I heard somethin'.'

'Naw,' Larry said, the fear of Henry's changing his mind evident in his croaky reply. 'Let's ride. This place is spookin' me somethin' awful.'

'Shuddup and let me listen!' Henry growled.

Spooked, the mare began to pull on the stunted tree to which Lane had hitched her. With every jerk of the reins, dry dust escaped from the rotten tree and it gave way a little more. Growing in confidence that she could achieve her goal, the mare's testing of the tree became more robust. She was still hidden from view, but that would not be for much longer. And spooked, once free she would likely bolt. He would have to try and unhitch the mare and calm her. But in doing so he would have to risk showing himself. From where he was, Lane could not judge how far he could venture without losing the protection of the overhang.

He heard the scrape of boot on the ridge above him.

One of the men, Henry, he reckond, had come to the edge of the ridge. Jack Lane could envisage him straining to see under the overhang.

'Let's get outta here, Henry,' Larry pleaded. 'I gotta real bad feelin' 'bout hangin' round.'

Jack Lane reached for the mare's reins but, her fright growing by the second, she pulled away. He dared not speak to coax her. If he could get his hands on the rifle in her saddle scabbard his chances of survival, should hostilities break out, would be greatly enhanced.

'Henry,' Larry whined. 'Let's make tracks.'

As he dared not risk upsetting the mare more than she already had been, Jack Lane had to settle for his sixgun as protection, consoling himself that even if he had got his hands on the rifle, with his lack of shooting skills it would not probably have mattered greatly. Being a farmer, he had never had the need that other men had to become gun-handy. No one ever saw a sodbuster as a threat.

'Henry,' Larry whined again.

'Will you be quiet!' Henry bellowed.

Jack Lane pondered on what he should do. His instinct was to break from cover and hope that surprise would make up for his lack of gun-handiness. Or should he wait and hope that Larry's continuous exhortations to move on would win out over Henry's suspicions.

If he broke from cover, there were paths down from the ridge either side of the hangover for Lane to worry about. He could not cover both paths simultaneously. So he could end up shooting at one man, leaving the second man free to act. And Jack Lane had no doubt that any advanatage he would gain by surprise would be quickly cancelled out. These men lived by their wits every second of every day, and would act instinctively to any threat to their well-being.

Not being a patient man, and truly believing that the man who acted first was the man who had the edge, Jack Lane decided to throw caution to the wind. He dived for the Winchester, grabbed it just as the mare broke free, and continued in a loping run to reach the cover of nearby boulders, rifle spitting more in hope than certainty. The boulders offered little protection from someone higher up, but they were the only cover around in the barren terrain. The scalp-hunters, used to reacting quickly, were almost immediately slinging lead at him, but it was sixgun lead and therefore not as accurate as rifle fire. Even so, as Jack Lane hunkered down in the boulders, several bullets buzzed close to him, and one that riocheted off a boulder close by to where he had landed took his hat with it. Another fraction lower and the top of his head would have been in the hat. He could not be certain of how many wild rounds he had fired during his madcap dash to cover, but every round from now on would have to have a definite target. Luckily, he had a full gunbelt, but he hoped that he would not have to get as close to the scalp-hunters as he would need to, to make a sixgun effective. Above him, the scalp-hunters had vanished off the ridge. As the sound of gunfire rolled away, he could hear urgent murmurings from the ridge – no doubt the scalp-hunters planning their attack.

The mare had broken free of the rotten tree but had calmed after her initial gallop. She was not too far away, but further than he liked.

The murmurings from the ridge became the loud exchanges of an argument.

'Well, I told ya we shouldn't hang round, didn't I,' Larry grumbled. 'It could be real dangerous tryin' to dislodge him from those boulders.'

'Shush!' Henry growled. 'I'm thinkin'. And I can't do that if you keep bleatin' like a damn sheep in my ear. Now can I?'

On hearing the angry dispute, Jack Lane's spirits lifted. Feuding between the scalp-hunters could only work to his advantage. However, the next exchange between the men replaced hope with despair.

'You better think real fast, Henry,' Larry bleated. ' 'Cause that dust cloud that was goin' east has changed direction and is comin' our way. And if them 'Paches catch us with their women's hair in our belts, we'll welcome a hasty toss into hell's fire.'

'We'd best dump the scalps, I reckon,' Henry said.

'Ain't no good doin' that. Those bloodthirsty bastards will smell their women from us. We got only one hope, and that's to get that fella's horse. Ain't it just our luck that the fettle of the nag we shot that man for ain't up to scratch.'

Other fella?

Jack Lane wondered if it was Ben Clark they were talking about? If it was, the bastards had murdered him for sure.

The wrangling between the pair returned to muted exchanges. Back to planning how they were going to dislodge him no doubt, Lane thought. Poking his head above the boulder behind which he was crouched, Lane only confirmed the hope-lessness of his situation. From where he was, the shooting angle was narrow and difficult for a skilled rifleman, but nigh on impossible for a fella of his even less than average competence. Were he to try to better his position, he would have to risk moving to decidedly poorer cover.

'Hello the boulders!' Henry called out. 'All we want is your nag, mister. If you don't raise no objections to us havin' your horse, me and Larry will let you be.'

'No deal,' Jack Lane said. 'Without a nag I'm a dead man anyway.'

'Well, I guess me and Larry's got to flush ya out, then.'

Jack Lane knew that he had one thing, and only one thing going for him. And that was that the murderous duo on the ridge did not know how ill-equipped he was to deal with them. He was counting on that they, having crossed paths with him in outlaw territory, would assume that he was of the same ilk as the other men who rode the deadly country. And that was the impression he had to convey to the scalp-hunters.

'You can try,' Lane flung back, with a heck of a lot more confidence than he was feeling.

A moment later disharmony again broke out between the scalp-hunters, and their exchanges bore a distinct note of panic.

'Them Indians are gettin' mighty close,' Larry groused.

'They ain't that close,' Henry countered. 'And they gotta find us first.'

'Ya know what 'Paches are like, Henry. They'll follow the sound of gunfire right to our door! There ain't no way to hide from an Apache. We gotta smoke him out fast!'

'How?' Henry asked petulantly.

'How the darn do I know. You're always claimin' to be the brains,' Larry groused. 'So you come up with a' idea.'

There was a lengthy silence before Henry spoke.

'I got me a real dandy idea,' he said, sounding pleased as punch.

The scalp-hunters returned to muttering. And when Larry spoke, he was gleeful.

'Always said you was a real clever cuss, Henry,' he said.

A moment later, crawling flat out on their bellies, the scalp-hunters made their way up the far side of the sloping ridge, making it impossible even with a mountain of luck, for Jack Lane to get off a telling shot. Alarmed, he reckoned he knew their destination. Balanced on the highest point of the ridge was a boulder that a determined effort could probably dislodge. And they could use the boulder as cover while they attempted to shift it. If they succeeded, Lane reckoned that he would be too preoccupied with the boulder's final destination as it thundered down off the ridge to give any consideration to retaliation. Stay put and he'd likely be flattened. However, break cover and the scalp-hunters would have a clear target to aim at.

Larry's generous praise for Henry's strategy was merited. Indeed, as Larry had said, Henry was a real clever cuss.

CHAPTER ELEVEN

Helpless to do very much about it, Jack Lane watched the pair creep up the slope of the ridge, steadily closing the gap between them and the boulder. He cut loose with a couple of token rounds, but knowing well what little risk there was to his adversaries, the scalp-hunters were untroubled by the gunfire. He could break from cover to try and nail them, but Lane knew that should he do so, the odds on success would be stacked heavily against him. And to try, he would have to expose himself to their return gunfire which would be a lot deadlier than any he could deliver. It was with a growing frustration that he watched their steady progress, unable to stop them from reaching their goal. Had the mare not broken free he could have risked mounting up and riding hell for leather with, he reckoned, a very good chance of putting distance between him and the scalp-hunters before they could respond.

When they reached the boulder the pair lost no time in levering it off the ridge. It rumbled down, its course erratic and ever-changing as it collided with other boulders, bouncing and weaving. There was no way of judging where the boulder would eventually come to rest until seconds before it did. Whichever way he tried to dodge the deadly missile, Jack Lane knew that his survival was in the lap of the gods. An added danger were the rocks and debris dislodged by the boulder. Even a stone of no great size dropping from a height would smash a skull.

Once the boulder was dislodged, there was a split second when the duo were exposed; in fact were sitting targets for a man handier with a gun than he was. But, determined to make the best of a bad situation, Lane cut loose with his Winchester. The taller of the pair, Henry, clutched at his side. The surprise of his moment's misfortune gave Lane the opportunity of getting off another round before he would have to decide on which way to leap to avoid ending up under the boulder. His second shot was even luckier than his first, and the tall scalp-hunter's concern with his side became a concern in the centre of his gut. He fell to his knees and then on to his face. The smaller of the men stood stock still for a second, not believing his eyes, and Lane cursed that he did not have the time to shoot again before leaping aside out of the path of the boulder's deadly rush. For a heart-stopping second, as the boulder was diverted one last time, it looked as though Jack Lane had chosen unwisely. But just as the boulder loomed over him, the merest brush against a jutting section of the rockface sent the boulder cartwheeling over him, a gigantic spinning ball. His luck held again. Someone was obviously beseeching the Lord for his safe return – Martha, he reckoned. The boulder crashed on to the sandier soil beyond the ridge's overhang, quickly losing its momentum, rolling to a harmless stop.

Lane dived under the overhang as a plethora of smaller rocks showered down in the boulder's wake. As he sought the refuge of the overhang he glanced up to the ridge above; Larry, the smaller of the scalp-hunters, had vanished. There were two tracks down from the ridge, one on either side of the hangover, to right and to left. Jack Lane turned towards the left side track, and knew that he had chosen wrongly on hearing a scatter of shale behind him. He swung round to find an evilly grinning Larry behind him, six gun cocked.

Lane was caught cold.

'Drop the rifle,' Larry ordered. 'Sixgun, too.' He sneered. 'Looks like you've plumb run outta luck, friend.'

Lane was counting his life in seconds when shale

spilled down from the ridge above him. The scalp-hunter called Henry had, by some miracle, got to his feet and was pointing a sixgun in no particular direction, his eyes burning with the fire of revenge. He pulled the trigger, using up his last ounce of energy to do so. He cut loose with one final agonized howl as the firing gun dipped and he shot himself in the foot. He toppled from the ridge, oblivious now to any pain as he crashed into the boulders below.

Jack Lane was the quicker to overcome his astonishment and he lunged at Larry. He rammed his head into the scalp-hunter's midriff driving the wind from him in a great whoosh. Lane's momentum slammed Larry against the rockface and the impact was fierce. Unluckily for Lane, his boots lost their purchase on the sandy soil and his legs went from under him. Taking full advantage of his good fortune, the scalp-hunter swung a boot that caught Lane on the side of the head. Stars exploded in front of Lane's eyes and a thousand bells started ringing in his ears, filling his head with their raucous cacophony. Before he could regain his wits, Larry moved with the instinctive swiftness of his breed and landed another boot in Lane's ribs. Forcing down the awful pain that racked his body, Lane grabbed the scalp-hunter's leg as he raised his boot again and twisted the limb as hard as he could. Larry cried out as his knee was dislocated. The injured leg became useless for standing on and he staggered back, hobbling. Advantage gained, Jack Lane ignored his pain to follow through with a hammer-hard fist to the side of Larry's face, which spun him like a top. As he came out of the spin Lane landed a second pile-driver in the scalp-hunter's gut that slammed him to the ground. A hunting knife flashed in the scalp-hunter's hand as if by magic, and Lane was fortunate to be able to cast himself aside to avoid landing on the upturned blade.

The awkward change of direction resulted in a heavy fall for Lane. With the speed of a mountain cat, Larry was riding on his back. He grabbed Jack Lane by the hair and yanked his head back, expos-ing his throat for the intended knife slash. Lane grabbed a fistful of dust. He threw it over his shoul-der in the scalp-hunter's face and elbowed him in the belly while he was preoccupied with the grit in his eyes. The scalp-hunter curled up enough for Lane to dislodge him with a heave. However, by the time he got to his feet, Larry had regained his composure and was readying himself to sling the knife. In the blink of an eye, Jack Lane spotted the scalp-hunter's sixgun where he had dropped it after he had crashed against the rockface. Lane dived for the gun. The knife whizzed past, only an inch wide of its target. Lane's fingers fumbled the pistol and it slid out of his reach, sliding over the shale to a midpoint between the men. Larry now dived for the sixgun also. Jack Lane reached. The scalp-hunter reached. Lane felt the gun in his hand with the scalp-hunter's face only feet away. Lane pulled the trigger. The force of the blast blew most of the scalp-hunter's head away.

Lane rolled away, weakened and disgusted by the awful violence. However, he knew that there was no time to lose. The Indians Larry had spoken of only minutes before, but it seemed a lifetime ago, were a deadly threat to his continued existence. Standing on legs that protested, he tucked the scalp-hunter's pistol inside his waistband, collected his own sixgun and rifle and hurried to where the mare was, wide-eyed and edgy. 'Easy, girl,' he coaxed the horse. 'It's only good old Jack.' The mare, recognizing the familiar voice, settled down. Mounting up, he told the mare, 'We've got to get out of here, pronto. I reckon that you would- n't fancy those Apache ponies too much, girl.' As if she understood, the horse set a fast pace away from the scene of carnage.

Jack Lane prayed that the distance he was putting between him and the Apaches would be enough for him to keep his hair. When they reached the ridge the Indians would find the two dead scalp-hunters. But they would also see the tracks which he had not had time to camouflage and, figuring that the fugitive was also a scalp-hunter, they would seek him out. 'We've got to eat up ground, horse,' he told the mare who, now that the immediate crisis was over, had lost her momentum. Or maybe the mare was just tuckered out and, if that were so, even with a head start he'd have a real problem trying to outrun the swiftly riding Apaches.

The insanity of his quest to rescue Lucas Watts's daughter came full blown to Jack Lane. A sodbuster. On board a third-rate nag. Used a gun with more hope than accuracy. Riding through Apache country. Pursuing, in Ike Durrel, one of the West's meanest killers.

'Shit, horse,' he swore. 'You've got a loco critter on your back, for sure!'

CHAPTER TWELVE

Going as far as he reckoned he could safely travel before the Indians reached the ridge and spotted him, Lane cut across rocky ground and turned into a narrow, short gully that he hoped would give him cover, and which would allow him to monitor the war party's direction once they came on from the ridge. He hoped that the rocky ground would confuse his trail, but he could not count on that, because the immediate sandy soil leading up to the harder ground had plenty of sign for the Indians to follow, and Apaches could read sign where no one else saw a thing. 'I reckon we're in for a hairy time, horse,' he said. 'And I want you to be real quiet.' The mare looked at him with what Jack Lane reckoned was pity.

Lane looked to the horizon, where the sun was beginning to dip. There was still at least an hour of daylight, he figured. Not long, but too long. How long would the Indians delay before riding on?

Maybe there would be some religious hocus-pocus to perform when they found their women's hair on the scalp-hunters, which would delay them? If night arrived before the Apaches, his chance of slipping away would be better. However, travelling in the desert at night might be every bit as dangerous and deadly as coming face to face with the Indians.

Jack Lane swore that if he got home with his skin intact and his hair still on his head, he would never again stray from behind a plough. He would stick to what he knew best, and not dabble in what he did not know about. Up to now he had used up a good deal of the cat's proverbial nine lives, and he could only wonder about how many of those fabled nine lives he had left.

He rolled a smoke, his first of a busy day. And through its smoke, he saw the first of the Apache riders arrive on the ridge. He checked anxiously on the dipping sun, and was disappointed that it did not seem to have moved and sunset would not come as quickly as he had reckoned it would. Back home on the farm, he could tell time almost to the minute by checking the position of the sun. But maybe the desert sun was trickier to read? Some shadows, he reckoned, had lengthened. However, it was a slow, languorous progress towards nightfall.

The Indians on the ridge were pointing downwards and gesticulating excitedly. Obviously they had spotted the dead scalp-hunters. The party quickly made their way down the tracks at either side of the overhang, absolute masters of their mounts. Several of them dismounted and converged on the scalp-hunters' bodies. One of the Apaches bent down and then straightened up, holding a scalp aloft. There were many angry gestures. One of the Apaches strode to the edge of the area immediately in front of the overhang and used his hand to shade his eyes, obviously scanning the country around for another presence. Only partly satisfied of its emptiness, he hurried back up to the ridge and repeated the exercise.

Jack Lane pulled the mare down on its side and sank down as deep as he could into the gully, but he felt that there was no gully deep enough to escape the Apache's searching eyes.

On hearing the rattle, he froze. Lane looked to his left to where a rattlesnake was sliding out from under a rock, well within spitting distance of where he lay. His first instinct was to leap up. His second instinct was to shoot the rattler. Both options would almost certainly bring him death. The third option, to remain perfectly still was no better. Death shone from the snake's evil beady eyes.

Jack Lane stretched out a slow, lazy hand to reach for a nearby stick with which to poke at the rattler in the hope that he could dissuade the snake from his evil intent, or use the stick to hook him away. He'd had enough of rattlers to last a lifetime. As he slowly extended the stick Lane was keenly aware that he was only a fang away from death.

The rattler reared its head, dodging the stick Lane was poking at him. But all he would have to do was misjudge the snake's weaving and it would be past the impeding stick to sink its fangs in him. As Lane was unable to hold on to the mare and deal with the rattler at the same time, the horse rolled away and galloped along the gully. Had the watching Apache seen the horse? Or would the rise of ground skirting their position give the mare cover? If it had, his luck was holding. But that would only be until the end of the gully where, if the mare continued on, she would lose the cover where the terrain flattened out.

Lane's preoccupation with what would inevitably be the result of the mare's breaking cover, if she had not already been spotted by the eagle-eyed Indian lookout, almost gave the rattler his chance. With the swiftness of a bullwhip unfurling, the snake cleverly curved its body round the tip of the stick and almost broke Lane's hold on it. He threw a rock at the rattler's head that forced the snake to loosen its grip on the stick giving Lane the chance to cast him away, not a great distance, but far enough for Lane to grab a second and bigger rock to hurl at the rattler. The rock bounced, fortunately, off the edge of the gully and got enough elevation to crash down on the snake. The rattler being stunned, Lane grabbed his chance to bring the heel of his boot down on the evil creature's head. He mashed the rattler's head under foot.

The snake was no longer a threat, but the need to kill the rattler had surely made him visible. Ducking back down into the gully, he checked on the ridge. The Apache lookout was gone. Jack Lane's frantic eyes swept the terrain, but there was no sign of the Indians. Where were they? Wherever the Indians had got to it made no difference, he realized with sudden gloom. Because without a horse he was stranded and as good as dead anyway. Horseless, the desert would claim him painfully and slowly.

Would he ever see his wife and unborn child again?

CHAPTER THIRTEEN

Jack Lane sat back, resigned, because there was nothing he could do. He had his Winchester. But with what he reckoned was at least a hundred Apaches in his neck of the woods, a single rifle would not be of much help.

The sun was now sitting like a tired old man on the not too distant hill towards which he had been riding. Beyond them he would reach the valley that Ike Durrel had returned to, to hide out until it was relatively safe for him to reappear. He regretted now that he had broken his journey to rest up and had not continued on to the hills where, had he done so, he might not be in the predicament he was in now.

Shadows crept into the gully. It would be night soon. Maybe he could slip away under cover of darkness? But Lane's hope was brief. Even if he did slip away, his progress on foot would be slow. Come sun-up he'd have the searing heat to deal with and the Apaches would still be on the prowl.

The sound of galloping horses slowly registered with Lane. Shod horses. Not Indian ponies. Whitemen! Moments later two riders rounded the tip of the rise of ground directly in front of the gully where Lane was hiding, riding low in the saddle, heads turning to look back every couple of seconds, their sixguns spitting lead. Lane was no expert in the use of guns, but even he could tell that riding helter-skelter the way the men were, and shooting backwards with a sixgun from a galloping horse, gave them a better chance of hitting the moon than downing any of their pursuers. To nail an Apache, under such adverse conditions, would take more luck than the riders appeared to be blessed with, having run into a bunch of bloodthirsty Indians in the vastness of the deseret.

'There's a gully over to your right, Dan!' the rider bringing up the rear shouted to the lead rider. 'Maybe we can make a stand.'

Lane tensed. The last thing he needed was for the pair to take refuge in the gully and bring Indians right to his door!

'A stand?' The lead rider exclaimed. 'There must be a hundred of them savages on our tails.'

'We ain't goin' to outrun 'em, that's for sure, Dan'

'It ain't that far to the hills, Luke,' the lead rider

called back. 'And once we reach them, it ain't too far more to the Durrel place. Ike and his brother are real pally with the Indians. As Ned Durell's guests, we'll be safe.'

Dan? Luke? The Rekton brothers?

'The legs are almost gone in these nags,' Dan shouted above the thunder of their horses as they drew nearer the gully. 'They'll never make it to the hills.'

'Damn it, Dan!' Luke bellowed. 'You take the gully if 'n you want. I'm stayin' in the saddle.'

Dan Rekton had no more than a couple of seconds' hesitation before he changed direction for the gully. An arrow followed him to the edge of the gully before it caught up with him and plunged between his shoulder blades. Rekton screamed and tried to clutch at the arrow. He lost control of his horse. The horse stumbled and threw Rekton. He went head first into the gully. Jack Lane's stomach turned over on hearing the snap of Dan Rekton's neck. The sickening crunch of shattering vertebrae filled Lane's mouth with sour bile.

Rid of its rider, the horse abandoned its charge and began to wander without direction as the charging Apaches kept up their pursuit of Luke Rekton, filling the gully with choking dust as they swept past.

Slowly, the stillness of the desert returned. Jack

Lane waited, allowing time for any Apache straggler to go past, before he poked his head above the rim of the gully. When he did, he seemed to be completely alone. And his good fortune was holding, because Dan Rekton's horse was close by. The mare came wandering back, too, drawn by the stallion's scent. Lane coaxed Rekton's horse, taking his time in putting the stallion at ease. The horse was still edgy and undecided about Lane. But when the mare came forward and nudged Lane, the stallion took the mare's friendliness as a reference and ambled over.

Jack Lane's good fortune knew no bounds. A couple of minutes ago, he'd been horseless and facing certain death. Now he had two mounts, which would make his journey a hell of a lot more comfortable. And there was a good chance that now he would not end up as a parcel of unknown bleached bones.

Discounting, of course, a bullet in the belly.

Darkness swept over the terrain and into the gully, bringing with it the night chill of the desert. But Jack Lane thought that, though the night would be cold, it would sure be a lot less cold than the death he had avoided; death which had seemed inevitable only a short time before.

When morning came, he ate half of his last portion of jerky and washed it down with water from Dan

Rekton's canteen which, to his relief, had been recently filled. The water tasted good. Food a man could go without in the desert, but water he could not. He had no shovel to dig a hole for Dan Rekton, and realistically it would have been unwise to waste time and risk a return visit from the Apaches. But he did take time to cover Rekton's body with stones. They would not give him much protection from marauding predators, but it was the best he could do.

His undertaking duties completed, Jack Lane saddled the stallion and emerged cautiously from the gully, the mare in tow. The dead man's rifle was still in its saddle scabbard and that was a gift worth having.

He rode towards the hills.

CHAPTER FOURTEEN

Where he could, Jack Lane made use of the terrain to shield himself from any watching eyes. However, he could only do so much to keep his presence a secret. Even being at his most careful, there were a million and one places from where he could be seen, and all he could do was hope that if there was a watcher, he'd be looking the other way while he drifted past.

Steadily, the hills got closer, and the desert heat became more and more intense to the point where he struggled to remain in the saddle, while the country around him shimmered and danced in the haze of heat coming up from the floor of the desert; a haze that dangerously distorted the lay of the land and tempted its guest to veer every which way in the hope of exhausting him and entrapping yet another victim to its cruel clutches. One

126

second the hills seemed only minutes away before the land shimmered again and the hills seemed unreachable, the desert's trick to make a weary man lose hope and surrender.

Jack Lane had never felt so weary.

Bone-tiredness, and the need to constantly monitor his surroundings slowed his progress to a crawl. For a time he never expected to make it to the burning hills, then his tired, sun-bleached eyes saw the first hint of a change in the baked earth. At first it was a little less bronzed, then greyish, and then the earth began to blacken and his farmer's eye recognized land that was becoming life-sustaining. A sudden, refreshing breeze had Jack Lane looking up at the hills which now seemed near enough to reach out and touch. And as he climbed into the hills the scraggly scrub changed to greener vegetation, and higher still to timber that would never earn any credit for its stoutness or sturdiness, but to many exhausted desert travellers its shade and cooler air must have renewed in them a hope that had almost turned to despair.

On reaching the top of a winding trail, Lane looked down in wonder at a green oasis that came as a complete surprise. Fickle nature had shunned the rock and sand of a couple of miles back for lush pasture nourished by a fissure in the far side of the hill from which sparkling clear water bubbled and flowed in a meandering course down the hill to feed a stream below that ran through the valley like glistening silver. The valley was not big, and by another cruel twist of fate he could see the barrenness of the desert beyond, to taunt and tease again a man whose journey was not at an end; his, he reckoned, was.

At the far end of the valley he saw grazing horses, and others in a corral which was close to a cabin that sat back like a hunched old man against a hill. A man came from the house to feed chickens in the yard, and Lane pulled back into the trees, reasoning that if he could see the man then he could in turn be seen.

Exhausted as he was, he was in no fit condition to attempt any rescue. Tiredness would go with rest, but waiting would do nothing to sharpen the other skills he would need to complete his mission to snatch Lucy Watts from Ike Durrel's clutches.

The chicken feeder was not Ike Durrel. The man was smaller and of a stumpy physique, whereas Ike Durrel had the slim form of a dancer. He had only had short sight of him as he blasted his way out of Arrow Bend after robbing the bank there, but there had been no mistaking his slim and elegant form.

The man, Lane guessed, would be Ned Durrel.

The chicken feeder turned towards the cabin to respond to something said to him. Another man appeared in the doorway, rolling a smoke. Narrow of hip and light of foot, he walked across the yard to join the man feeding the chickens. He lit the smoke and puffed leisurely on the weed, like a man who hadn't a care in the world. And if any came along, was confident enough to reckon that he could deal with any trouble thrown his way.

Ike Durrel.

Finding Durrel was one thing – dealing with him was an entirely different matter. A woman came from the blind side of the cabin bearing a wash-basket. The long mane of coal-black hair, almost waist-length, identified her as Emily Watts. However, there was something not quite right about what he was looking at. But Lane could not put his finger on what was odd about the set-up.

A storm sprang up out of nowhere, as storms in the desert sometimes do. One minute the sky was clear, except for a couple of drifting clouds, then, in minutes, the clouds darkened and merged and moved across the sky in a dark mass of rain and thunder. Lightning streaked across the sky and came to dance on the floor of the valley and the desert around, and stabbed fingers of blinding light at the hills, starting several small fires that Jack Lane hoped would not join up to make the hills an inferno which he would have to abandon in double quick time, losing the benefit of their cover in the process.

A solid sheet of rain drenched Lane in seconds,

and after the heat of the afternoon it was like cold fingers of ice poking at his skin. Lightning felled a tree near him, igniting other trees and scrub. Fortunately, a sudden increase in the intensity of the rain quenched the blaze almost as soon as it had started. Other fires too fizzled out, filling the hills with air-sucking black smoke. The storm was brief and furious. Within twenty minutes the sky had cleared. The storm raced away, breaking and scattering in different directions. For a dreaded moment, the tail end of the storm curled back, fickle of nature as desert storms were, but it spun away and was swept back into the storm. The storm left a gloom behind that quickly became twilight. Lamps were lit in the cabin windows. A half-dozen Apaches with a string of wild horses in tow arrived at the cabin to parley. Earthenware jugs were exchanged for the horseflesh. The Indians rode away, slugging down moonshine. The Durrel brothers corralled the horses and went back inside. A lone fiddle struck up, playing a tune that Lane had heard before, a plaintive Irish lament that haunted the intensifying darkness. Lane wondered which of the brothers had the ability to make the fiddle almost human in its keening.

The lonely sound filled the twilight; the kind of sound that made a man think of loved ones and home. A melancholy seeped through Jack Lane and, when the fiddler struck up an Irish jig, he was pleased that he had chosen a cheerier rhythm.

Later, Jack Lane made his way down to the valley and edged along a jutting rock that would hide him from curious eyes for most of the way to the cabin. His purpose was to reconnoitre and not rescue. However, if the opportunity to spirit Emily Watts away presented itself, he would be a fool not to take it. As he crept past the corral the horses became restless, and he was just in the nick of time to dive into a shadow when the cabin door was flung open and Ike Durrel emerged, ears cocked and eyes scanning the yard. The fiddle stopped playing. Now he knew that it was not Ike Durrel who was the fiddle-player. And it seemed incongruous that his stumpy-framed brother should have music such as he had played in his soul.

'Anyone out there?' Ike Durrel called out.

'Prob'ly them horses the Indians traded that's spookin' the others,' Ned called out from inside the cabin. 'Nothin' like the smell of an Apache to make a horse nervous.'

The fiddle started up again, playing a polka. Ike Durrel took a couple of paces into the yard and stood listening.

'Stop that caterwaulin', Ned,' he called back to the house.

'Like I told ya, Ike,' Ned Durrel hollered,

annoyedly. 'It's them Apache ponies.' He began to play again.

'Damn fiddle!' Ike Durrel growled sourly. He went back inside, bad-temperedly slamming the door fit to bring the cabin down round them.

Jack Lane let his breath out slowly, and wiped away the perspiration that had broken on his forehead. He crept from the shadows and went forward cautiously. There was not a lot he could achieve from his visit other than to learn the topography round the cabin and get the feel of the place. He noted several nooks and crannies where, if the need arose, he might take shelter from flying lead.

Seeing a glow of lamplight from the far side of the cabin, he made his way there. Crouched under the window he edged an eye up and saw Emily Watts sitting on the edge of a bed in what was a clean and well-furnished room. It puzzled him to find Ike Durrel's kidnap victim in such pleasant surroundings, but he was pleased that Emily had not seemingly suffered the fate which he had feared. He was about to tap on the window when the room door opened and Ike Durrel entered. Before he ducked below the window, he saw Emily Watts spring off the bed. It looked as though Emily's reaction to Durrel's appearance indicated that, though she was living in relative comfort, she was still Durrel's prisoner, and probably a whole lot more besides.

Lane heard the door of the cabin open and tensed. Footsteps crossed the porch and then dulled as they reached the earth of the yard. Lane crept to the corner of the cabin and cast an eye to the yard. Ned Durrel was contentedly smoking a pipe, oblivious to the presence of an interloper.

The lamplight from Emily Watts' bedroom went out. Jack Lane's mind filled with the horrors that were probably being visited on Emily, and he cursed that he had not arrived earlier in time to whisk her away.

After a couple of minutes Ned Durrel stretched and made to return inside. To be on the safe side, Lane moved back a couple of paces from the corner of the cabin and froze when, clumsily, the heel of his boot knocked against a tin bucket.

Ned Durrel stopped dead in his tracks.

The noise was not significant, but in the stillness of the night it did not need to be. Jack Lane stood stock-still willing Ned Durrel to continue on. But it was not to be. Durrel's pause had been to give him time to pinpoint from where the sound had come. And now that he had, he drew his pistol and came Lane's way.

Lane hurried back to the darkness at the far end of the cabin, hoping that when Ned Durrel came and checked, the darkness would be black enough to engulf him. However, if Ike Durrel had heard and relit the bedroom lamp to come and investigate, the spill of light would likely breach the darkness enough to reveal him.

And he had another worry.

A full moon was coming from behind a bank of cloud left over from the earlier storm. The moon's progress was lazy, but was it slow enough? If the full moon broke from behind the clouds, there would be nowhere left for Jack Lane to hide.

CHAPTER FIFTEEN

Ned Durrel appeared at the edge of the cabin, sixgun cocked and pointing. Squinting, he peered into the darkness. The full moon edged from behind the clouds and sent a shaft of clear bright light across the yard behind Durrel and racing towards where Jack Lane was hiding. The lamp in the bedroom had not been relit. Lane reckoned that Ike Durrel was much too busy to be bothered. However, the absence of the lamplight would not matter a jot. Moonlight would reveal him any second now.

Jack Lane slid his pistol from its holster. Once Ned Durrel spotted him he would be left with no choice but to shoot.

As a maverick cloud swept across its face, the beam of moonlight vanished. But it was only a temporary relief. All he could do was wait, not daring to move a muscle, and hope that Ned Durrel's curiosity would be satisfied before the moon returned. When it did, it was likely, bearing in mind its swift progress before the cloud cover hindered its light, that its beam would mercilessly expose him.

Lane drew a bead on Ned Durrel with his Colt .45. At that moment, if another man was holding the gun, Durrel would be a dead man standing. However, though it was a close and easy shot to make, Lane knew that his lack of expertise would probably make all the difference and hand Durrel the opportunity to shoot back.

And Jack Lane doubted very much that Ned Durrel would miss.

The crash of a corral post and the sudden movement of horses sensing trouble diverted Ned Durrel's attention.

'Damn Apache nags,' he swore, hurrying to shoo the horses trying to escape back into the corral.

Jack Lane could not believe his good fortune. If there was such a thing as a guardian angel, he sure was overworked trying to save his hide. Taking advantage of the commotion, Lane slipped away into the night, chased by the moon, thankful that so far he had not been discovered, and the rescue of Emily Watts was still possible.

Lane woke from a restless slumber, still struggling to come up with a plan to snatch Emily Watts from

Ike Durrel's clutches, as he had been before he went to sleep. He had had a vague plan that he could have rescued Emily by stealth, with a great dollop of luck, of course. But now in the cold light of day he gave up on that idea, and was left with no idea at all.

'That's how much of a darn greenhorn you are, Jack Lane,' he grumbled.

He rolled out of his bedroll, his stomach rubbing against his backbone from lack of grub, and went to the edge of a promontory overlooking the valley in the hope that by some magical means a solution would present itself. It did not. It was just after sun-up, but Ned Durrel was already up and about and attending to chores. The positioning of the cabin was cleverly done, in a way that all approaches to it could be watched. Any rider coming in would be seen from a good distance off. As the morning drew on, Jack Lane's despondency grew as several half-baked schemes went south one after the other, and no plan of action presented itself. In fact it became starkly obvious that, even with a dozen riders coming in, the Durrels could give a very good account of themselves, if they were not outright winners. The long, wide-open approaches to the cabin would prove murderous under a hail of unimpeded lead from the cabin. But, Jack Lane's brow furrowed thoughtfully, a lone rider of an unthreatening demeanour might get close to the cabin – with any luck, right up to the cabin. He was unknown to the Durrels. So he could ride in as a stranger seeking to refill his canteen. Once there, Emily Watts would recognize him, would guess the reason for his arrival, and would, he hoped, get an opportunity to assist in her rescue.

Jack Lane's spirits lifted. He had a plan – well, a plan of sorts. And one that might just work, too.

Of course there was a fly in the ointment. There always was. And that was that the Durrels might err on the side of caution, reckon that the lone rider might be a hole-in-the-head badge-toter seeking a reputation for nailing Ike Durrel, and shoot in preference to finding out the identity and purpose of their visitor. Ike Durrel would certainly not take any chances, Lane figured. So that left him counting on Ned Durrel who, according to Ben Clark, was not cut from the same cloth as his meaner brother.

He saddled up and rode down into the valley, brazen as you like. Soon, Ned Durrel saw him and stopped doing his chores to watch the incoming rider with interest. He strolled back to the cabin porch and picked up a rifle. Laying it across his chest he came forward. Every instinct in Jack Lane was to turn tail while there was still enough distance between him and Ned Durrel to give him a fair chance of avoiding lead. And when Ned

Durrel dropped the rifle to a shooting position, a sweat as thick as treacle broke on Lane; a sweat that had nothing at all to do with the desert heat, but everything to do with a bone-shaking fear.

From Ned Durrel's perspective, the stranger had to be either an innocent gone astray (and there weren't many innocents abroad in country shared by Apaches and outlaws), or a friend of Ike's seeking refuge or making a social visit, either of which he would not welcome. The idea of the incoming rider being a lawman was laughable and not worth considering, unless he was a badge-toter with scattered marbles. Of course, there were others as well as the law who had scores to settle with his brother. So maybe he should just down the rider and be done with it. If the man was a friend of Ike, he'd cry no tears anyway.

Strangely, having come from the same womb, Ned Durrel did not share in Ike's wayward life; breaking horses and trading them was what he liked to do. But Ike was kin, his younger brother, and he had always provided refuge for him. He would defend him, too. And this time, should trouble come, it would be no different.

'Ike,' he hollered. 'Get yourself out here. Now!'

CHAPTER SIXTEEN

Drawing close to the cabin, the urge to turn tail and ride as fast as the wind was almost irresistible. Jack Lane knew that living on luck as he had been doing, he might very well have tried Lady Luck's indulgence a mite too much, fickle lady that she was. And he also knew that with his indifferent shooting skills, going up against the likes of the Durrel brothers was about as loco a thing as he could do. A small voice inside his head kept telling him that, under the circumstances, were he to turn tail it would simply be good sense and not cowardice. But then every coward there ever was told himself the same thing.

Ike Durrel came from the cabin, pulling up his trousers and buckling on his gunbelt. He came to stand alongside Ned Durrel to vet the incoming rider.

'Don't recognize his gait, Ned. Law, you reckon?'

'Can't see no lawman with that big a hole in his head,' was Ned Durrel's opinion. 'Prob'ly some hobo who's lost his way.'

'Gimme the rifle,' Ike said. 'No point in taking chances.'

Ned Durrel was uneasy with his younger brother's request. Though he lived in a land where death was always in the next shadow, he had always only killed when there was nothing else he could do to save himself.

'One rider ain't goin' to be no trouble,' Ned said. 'And if he is, he won't be for long. No point, that I can see, in killin' a man without cause, Ike.'

Ike Durrel laughed meanly.

'That, brother, is what'll get you lead in the belly some day,' he opined. 'Now, gimme the 'Chester, Ned.' Ike Durrel snorted. 'How the hell you've managed to survive out here for the last fifteen years beats me, Ned.'

'I put it down to fair play, Ike.'

Ike Durrel's contempt for his brother was scathing.

With a short distance to go, Jack Lane could see the tussle of wills between the brothers. It looked as though Ned Durrel was at odds with his brother and that gave him new hope. As he arrived in the

141

yard the disagreement ended and the Durrels' concentration was focused on Lane.

'Howdy,' Lane greeted the brothers, and got only sour-faced looks in response. 'The desert seems to have fooled me, gents. I need a pointer, if you'd oblige. Maybe a full water canteen and a bite to eat as well. Sure appreciate it.'

'Where you headed, stranger?' Ned Durrel enquired.

'Border bound,' Lane replied.

'Well, you'll reach the border pretty much on any trail going south from here,' Ned said.

'That's if you manage to keep your hair,' Ike Durrel added. 'Don't recall seein' you before, mister.'

'I guess that's 'cause you ain't,' Lane said, hoping that Ike Durrel wouldn't take umbrage at his slightly impudent response. Maybe he should grovel some, but if he was going to die in the next couple of seconds, he did not want to go out cringing.

'Someone doggin' your tail, friend?' Ike Durrel enquired of Lane.

Jack Lane leant on his saddle horn and chuckled. 'Couldn't rightly say, mister. Just let's say that if there ain't, there should be.'

'Law?' Ike Durrel pressed.

'Could be anyone of a bevy of *hombres*,' Lane said. 'But lead is lead from wherever it comes. So I need to reach Mexico, pronto. Maybe travel on to the South Americas for a spell. Give folk a chance to forget about Jack Lane.'

'Never heard of no Jack Lane,' Ike Durrel growled.

'Ever been down Montana way?' Lane asked.

'Montana? You're a heck of a long way from home,' Ned Durrel observed.

Jack Lane grinned. 'Coupla posses kinda mapped my trail for me, mister.' He looked to the cabin, hoping to catch sight of Emily Watts, but she was nowhere to be seen. 'Any hope of that grub I was talking about?'

Ike Durrel snorted. 'This ain't no hotel!'

'I'll just fill my canteen, then.'

'Well, ain't that right bad luck,' Ike Durrel scoffed. 'Well's just gone bone dry.'

Ike Durrel's attitude pitched Jack Lane into a quandary. Riding on was not on the cards, because a return visit was out of the question. He had survived up to now against the wishes of Ike Durrel, he reckoned. If he came back that would not be the case. He had one chance to try and rescue Emily Watts.

And one chance only.

'Has your nag grown roots, friend?' Ike Durrel snarled, when Lane had not immediately acted on his dismissal.

Fortunately Ned Durrel was in a kinder mood

than his brother was. Though his acquaintance with Ned Durrel was only minutes old, Jack Lane figured that he was a couple of notches above Ike in character.

'The well's round back,' Ned said. 'When you've filled your canteen come inside the house and I'll rustle up something to fill the hole in your belly.'

'Like I said, Ned,' Ike growled. 'This ain't no hotel!'

There was a tense stand-off between the brothers which Ned Durrel won. Ike Durrel stormed off to the cabin.

'Hope I ain't brewing trouble for you, friend?' Lane said.

Ned Durrel laughed humorously. 'Trouble shared my cradle, mister. Ain't never gone far 'way since.' He turned and followed Ike to the cabin.

Jack Lane dismounted, took his canteen and went behind the house to the well, keeping a keen eye open for Emily Watts. But she was still not to be seen. He filled the canteen, returned leisurely and hung it on his saddle horn. The more time he could waste, the greater the chance of Emily seeing him. If she had not put in an appearance by the time he had partaken of whatever Ned Durrel put in front of him, he would ask for a bucket for his horse to drink from, the poor critter needed it anyway. By then if he had not caught sight of Emily

Watts he would have a real dilemma.

'Apache pony,' Ned Durrel said, slapping a plate of meat down on the table in front of Lane. 'All we've got. Take it or leave it.'

'Thanks. Looks good.'

Ned Durrel went to the dresser and came back with a jug of moonshine. 'Can be tough. A slug or two should help get it down your gullet.'

'Thanks.'

Lane had the jug to his lips when, over its rim, he saw Emily Watts coming from the bedroom he had been looking into the previous night, tying back her long mane of black hair with a strip of rawhide. How would she react. To Jack Lane's surprise, she paused for just a sliver of a second before asking Ike:

'And who would this be?'

'Says his name is Jack Lane,' Ike replied, sourly.

'Well, howdy, Mr Lane,' Emily greeted Lane, offering her hand to shake. She looked at his plate. 'Apache pony. Tough as nails.'

'Right now I'm so hungry I'd eat stones, ma'am,' Lane said.

With her back turned to the Durrel brothers, her eyes met Lane's.

'Eat up and be on your way,' Ike Durrel snarled, jealous of Emily's welcome for the stranger.

'Surely,' Lane said. He stood up. 'Mind if I unbuckle to get this down?' His question was directed to Ned Durrel.

'Makes sense, I guess.'

Jack Lane unbuckled his gunbelt and lay it on the table near him, the sixgun at his fingertips. Ned Durrel, he might outdraw. But there was no chance of beating Ike Durrel to the draw. He was hoping that when he used the Colt, any minute now, Ike Durrel would be stunned enough to slow his lightning-fast hands.

'Nice gun, Mr Lane,' Emily Watts said, sliding the sixgun from its holster.

'Nice?' Ike Durrel laughed. 'That's the lousiest piece of junk I ever seen, woman!'

Jack Lane could not understand why Emily Watts had acted the way she had, unless she was of a mind to shoot Ike Durrel herself. But he wished she would just put the gun back on the table, because Ike Durrel was bent over with laughter and the chance to get the drop on him would never be better. Then in a flash of insight, Jack Lane knew why Emily Watts had taken the gun. And his insight was confirmed when she turned the sixgun on him.

'Move and I'll kill you, Mr Lane,' she said, with a viper-like attitude that was completely at odds with the woman he had known back in Arrow Bend only a short time ago. 'This man has come to take me back to my father, Ike. Isn't that so, Mr Lane?'

Jack Lane's eyes popped when Emily Watts cuddled up to Ike Durrel.

'Ike and I met on the train when I paid a visit to my Aunt Helen back East a couple of months ago. It was then that I came up with the idea of Ike robbing Father's bank. And to make it look like I had been kidnapped, when all the time I was craving to be with Ike.

'There was no other way that I could be with Ike, Mr Lane. My father would never have accepted him as his son-in-law.'

'It would be a kind of strange thing, sure enough,' Jack Lane said. 'A banker with a bank robber for a son-in-law.' Then curious, he asked, 'How come a woman reared so delicately could fall for a—'

'A what?' Ike Durrel reacted maliciously.

Jack Lane had already decided that the strange turn of events had done for him anyway, so he said, 'Toerag, like you, Durrel.'

Ike Durrel's hand dropped to his sixgun. Emily Watts stayed his hand.

'I'm not sure that killing Mr Lane would be right, Ike,' she said.

'Not sure? Hah! He came here to take you back to your pa, and probably kill me for takin' you from him in the first place. In my book, they're good reasons for blowin' his head clean off his shoulders, Em'ly.'

'Mr Lane could take word back to my father about how you and I are in love, Ike. And that that's the way I want it to be.'

'Are you loco?' was Ike Durrel's fiery response. 'Your pa would set the hounds of hell loose on me.'

'Ike's right, Em'ly,' Ned Durrel said. 'You made your choice when you chose my brother—'

'Sounds to me like you figure she didn't make the right choice, Ned,' Ike growled.

'You didn't, Ike,' Ned flung back. 'The kind of trail you ride ain't a fittin' one for someone like her. Her ways and yours won't mix good. If you wanted a woman as a wife, then you should have picked a woman of your own kind.'

'That's real insultin', Ned.'

Ike Durrel's mood was as mean as a spitting rattler, and there was anger bursting through every pore of his body.

'What I said is true, Ike. I say let the woman ride back to her pa with Lane.'

'I don't want to,' Emily said. 'Can't you all get it through your thick skulls that I love Ike?'

'A woman such as her,' Ned stabbed a finger at Emily, 'will always have someone lookin' for her, Ike. You can kill this fella and the next, and the one after that maybe, too. But there'll always be another down the line. Trouble always waitin' in the wings.'

Ned Durrel's stance became granite hard.

'When you come here in future, Ike,' he declared, 'you come alone. Understood?'

Ike Durrel's anger peaked. His sixgun flashed from leather, and before Ned Durrel could react Ike put a bullet dead centre between his eyes. Taking advantage of the confusion, weaponless, Jack Lane leaped at Ike Durrel, his fists already swinging, the right one of which smashed the hardcase's nose. Durrel spun backwards, howling. Lane grabbed the chair he had been sitting on and broke it on Durrel. The outlaw staggered about, his eyes rolling. Lane made ready to put every ounce of muscle he had into the next and what he reckoned would be the final blow but froze on hearing Emily Watts's threat.

'Leave him be, or I'll kill you, Mr Lane. Now, we'll wait until Ike regains his wits. Then I'll do exactly what he wants.'

'Does that include murder?'

'Yes, it does,' she stated bluntly.

'What evil's got into you, Emily?' Lane asked, bemused.

'Howdy, ma'am.' Surprises were coming thick and fast. Ben Clark's roughhouse visage was at the open window, a rifle pointing at Emily. 'Drop the gun. Don't want to shoot a woman. But if I have to, I will.'

There was no mistaking the ring of truth in

Clark's threat.

'Drop it,' he repeated.

Emily did as he had instructed. Ike Durrel was of another mind and dived for the sixgun he had dropped during Lane's onslaught. He grabbed Emily to use as a shield.

'Ike,' Emily pleaded, bewildered by Durrel's action.

'Shuddup!' he growled. 'I ain't headed for no gallows. Ned was right, anyway. You ain't my kinda woman. Drop the 'Chester through the window and your sixgun, too,' he ordered Clark.

There was a sliver of a chance for Jack Lane to act, and he took it. He grabbed the knife Ned Durrel had used to carve the horsemeat with. 'Duck your head, Emily,' he shouted. Her eyes having been opened to Ike Durrel's duplicitous and coyote nature, she did not hesitate to comply with Lane's request. A second later the knife was stuck in Durrel's throat. Grasping at the blade, he staggered back, the gurgling sound of blood flooding his lungs in his throat. He crashed to the floor and lay still.

'Heck,' Ben Clark exclaimed. 'Figured that when you left Huntley I'd tag along but keep my nose out until you needed help. But you sure learn fast, friend. And,' his gaze went to Durrel, 'you sure as hell deliver tough justice.'

Emily Watts went and stood over Ike Durrel and

spat in his upturned face. Jack Lane went and put a comforting arm round her shoulder.

'Time to go home, Emily,' he said, soothingly.

CHAPTER SEVENTEEN

Setting out from the cabin after burying the Durrel brothers, Jack Lane knew that the journey home would likely be every bit as dangerous as the outward journey had been. Indians were still on the prowl, so were a whole host of other evil-minded critters who would, if they caught sight of the shapely Emily Watts, see the potential for pleasure and profit. The Apaches, too, would like a white female trophy to parade.

'You know, Jack,' said Ben Clark, coming alongside. 'I reckon that we can take a lead from those three wise fellas in the Good Book and take a different way home. We'll swing down towards the border, along a little known trail I've travelled a time or two, and then wind back to Huntley.'

The news should have lifted Jack Lane's spirits sky high, but there was one thing that dampened his spirits, and that was the little matter of the Hoddsville bank loot which he had counted on retrieving on his way home.

'Looks like I ain't given you good news, Lane,' Clark observed. Then he laughed.

'What's so funny?' Jack Lane enquired.

'Your face, Lane.'

'What's wrong with it?'

'It's got a big sign on it that reads: Hoddsville.' Jack Lane came ramrod straight in the saddle. 'Real clever thinking, stashing that bank loot under that fella. Nice touch, too, warning folk off with a message about him having died of fever.'

Clark patted his bulging saddlebags.

'But the lawman in me figured that the loot should be returned to its lawful owners – the Hoddsville Bank. And don't be downcast. I figure there'll be a reward.'

Resigned, Jack Lane said, 'I'd probably have taken it back myself anyway.'

'Well, I thought it was best to keep temptation out of your way and keep you an honest man, Jack.'

'You're a real guardian angel, ain't you,' Lane groaned.

There were many detours to avoid trouble before Huntley appeared below them when they came through a gap in the hills above the town. Ben

Clark was as good as his word, and had seen them safely through the hostile country between Ned Durrel's horse ranch and Huntley. News of Ike Durrel's demise, for which Ben Clark gave Jack Lane full credit, came as both a shock and a surprise to the inhabitants of the outlaw-infested town. And during the couple of days he spent there to rest up at Clark's house before completing the last leg of his journey back to Arrow Bend, the hardcases stepped aside to let Lane pass, some even going so far as to tip their hat, if not out of respect then out of a desire not to upset the man who had made one of the most evil and toughest *hombres* in their league, wormbait.

'You've become quite a celebrity, Jack,' Clark said.

'I can live without their kudos,' Lane replied. 'All I want from now on is to love my woman and my kid and plough the sod. I've had enough of hard riding and tough justice to do me for a lifetime and more.'

They were sitting on the porch with the rising moon slanting its light across them.

'I figure that me and Emily will be homeward bound on the morrow,' Lane said, sad that he was parting company with a man whom he now called a friend, and for whom his respect had grown enormously since their first meeting. It was obvious that Ben Clark had not yet overcome his

154

demons to the point where he could tame them, but Lane reckoned that he was a long way along a hard road, and had acquired most of the resolve he would need to complete the journey. And he was pleased to see in Clark's eyes the disappointment of a friend leaving.

'It's been quite an adventure, Jack,' Clark said.

'Not to mind an eye-opener to boot,' Lane laughed. 'I've learned a good lesson, Ben. A man should stick to doing what he knows best how to do.'

'That's a wise philosophy, sure enough,' said Clark, thoughtfully.

'If you're ever round Arrow Bend way, drop by the farm,' Lane invited.

'I'd like to do that,' Clark promised sincerely.

As he approached Arrow Bend, Jack Lane drew rein to talk to Emily Watts who, during the long trek to Huntley and from there to Arrow Bend, had not had many words to say. Lane could understand Emily's silence. The last time she had been in Arrow Bend she had been a young girl full of the promise of love (although how she could have loved a toerag like Ike Durrel was a mystery), and she was returning as a woman who had been hurt by the cruelty and disappointment of life.

'Emily,' Jack Lane began, 'I know it ain't going to be easy to forget, and harder still to see any hope in the future. But what happened back at the Durrel place need never be known. If you can keep the secret, I can, too.'

Jack Lane was pleased by the gleam of hope that glowed in Emily Watts's eyes.

'I rescued you from Ike Durrel's evil clutches and restored you to your pa,' Lane said. 'That's my story, Emily. And I don't see any reason why that shouldn't be yours, too.'

'Thank you, Mr Lane,' Emily said. 'You're a good and a fine man.'

Lane laughed. 'There's a couple of us around, Emily. And I'm certain that some day soon, you'll find one.'

A man called Harry Larch was feeding his chickens as they rode by on the outskirts of Arrow Bend and, seeing them, checked in awe, 'Is that you, Jack Lane? Or am I lookin' at your ghost?'

'It's me, Harry,' Lane called back.

'Doggone. And you've got Miss Watts with ya.'

'That was the plan when I set out, Harry.'

Larch dropped the bucket he was feeding the chickens from and ran ahead, shouting at the top of his voice as a witness would have done in the Holy Land when the Saviour had cleansed a leper. By the time they reached town, Jack Lane and Emily Watts were greeted by an awestruck crowd, none more awestruck than Charlie Brady.

'Jack Lane,' he said. 'You're a sight for sore eyes, my friend.'

Lucas Watts came from the bank, paused for a second to pinch himself, and then ran along the main street to meet his daughter who, equally glad to see her father, met him halfway, tears streaming down both their faces.

'This calls for a celebration,' Brady said.

Jack Lane shook his head. 'I'll do my celebrating at home, Charlie.'

'Tomorrow we'll split a bottle,' Brady said.

'Tomorrow,' Lane agreed, riding on.

It was the following autumn after a rich harvest had been taken in, when Jack Lane saw a rider approaching. He had seen the man's saddle gait before and his heart sang out at the prospect of a visit from Ben Clark.

Stories about Huntley having a tough lawman who had restored the town to one of law and order had spread far and wide. Jack Lane called to the house for his wife to join him. 'Bring the boy, too,' he said. 'I want my old friend to see the fine son you gave me, Martha.'

As he came near, Ben Clark's spirits soared at seeing the happy family gathering awaiting him in front of a house made from spanking new lumber. Jack Lane's joy was complete when he saw a clean-shaven, fresh-faced man with all the greyness of his former addiction gone. And his joy knew no bounds when he saw the star pinned to Ben Clark's shirt.

'Got my old job back,' Clark said proudly. 'Huntley is a family town again, Jack.' He opened his saddlebag and took a bulging cloth sack from it and handed it to Jack Lane. 'That's five thousand dollars, Jack,' he said. 'The reward for that stolen money you returned to the Hoddsville Bank.'

The sun slid down behind the purple hills at the boundary of Jack Lane's extended farm on the third happiest day of his life. The first had been the day he had held Martha, when he thought that he never would again. And the second had been when he had witnessed the marvel of creation from inside her.

'Come inside the house, Ben,' Jack Lane invited Clark. 'And as the Irish would say, a thousand welcomes, friend. Oh, and by the way.' He took the boy proudly in his arms. 'This fella's name is Ben, too,' he said.